To: Jan
With Love
Shelley xxx

A Parallel Persona

S.J. Gibbs

Copyright © 2021 S.J. Gibbs

All Rights Reserved. No part of this publication may be reproduced, stored in a retrieval system, or transmitted, in any form or by any means, electronic, mechanical, photocopying, recording or otherwise without the prior consent of the author.

This novel is a work of fiction. The names, characters and incidents portrayed in it are the work of the author's imagination. Any resemblance to actual persons, living or dead, or events that have occurred are entirely coincidental.

ISBN: 9798519016223

DEDICATION

For Sophie and Charlotte

With Love

S.J. GIBBS

ACKNOWLEDGEMENTS

The author would like to acknowledge the support of her fellow writers and members of JAMS Publishing: Michael Andrews, who did the formatting for publication, and J.M.McKenzie for her valued and continued support. Also AJ Jones who did the proofreading and editing.

She would also like to acknowledge the patience and encouragement of her husband, Steve, and all her family and friends.

Chapter 1

Alison Ware was full of regret that she hadn't called her dad the night before he suffered a fatal heart attack. As her 30th birthday approached, this wasn't all that she regretted in life. She regretted not having followed her heart and allowing her own limited expectations to define her life and decisions. It was almost as if she was too afraid to live.

She looked around her basement flat. It was cramped and windowless, made to feel even darker and smaller by the low ceilings. It was stuffy, warm and airless, and she was still not used to the sewage smell that permeated her tiny sitting room. She chewed on the tasteless, last piece of reheated, rubbery pizza that was left over from the night before.

What had become of her? She'd dreamed of opening her own restaurant, but here she was, eating the remnants of last night's take-away.

She was exhausted, her back hurt and her nerves were frayed.

She hated her miserable job as a waitress; every day was a bad day. Why couldn't she pluck up the courage to quit? But if she did, what was the alternative? She relied on the money to pay the bills, but surely there was more to life than what she currently had.

Her head throbbed so she took a couple of painkillers: the last two in the pack. She would need to buy more, but hadn't she only bought a pack of 16 a couple of days ago?

The negative thoughts continued to buzz around her head. When did she last laugh out loud? She couldn't remember. She didn't see her friends anymore. But did she even have any? How was it that everybody else seemed to be doing well in their lives and she'd ended up in this rut? Maybe it was time to listen to that little voice inside her and do something about it.

Looking around the room again, she decided that a good place to start would be to clean up her immediate surroundings. The dust on her furniture was thick, and she found it surprisingly therapeutic to start removing it with a duster and some polish. She stripped her bed and vacuumed her mattress, dreading to think what might have been inhabiting it. Then, she vacuumed all of her carpets.

Feeling motivated, she turned to face herself in the bathroom mirror. What had she become? Her eyebrows looked like two giant moustaches. She grabbed her tweezers and plucked away until they finally had some shape. She showered and applied some body lotion to her skin, blow-dried her long, straggly hair, filed her fingernails, cut her toenails and applied a deep-pink nail polish to both. Rummaging through her wardrobe, she selected the cleanest clothes she could find: navy-blue jeans and a cream, V-necked jumper. She sorted the rest of her clothes into coloureds and whites. Everything needed washing. She put on the first wash and poured some fabric conditioner into the washing machine. The smell of lemons gave her a momentary sense of relief against the overpowering stench of sewerage.

Her thoughts raced ahead so fast that she struggled to process them. She lit a cigarette to try and calm herself, knowing that soon the terrible thoughts inside her head would start, and as usual she wouldn't be able to switch them off. Her mind was like a whirlwind, out of control. She lay on her freshly made bed, paralysed by despair, knowing she would not be able to do anything to stop it from happening. Tears trickled down her cheeks. The black clouds were already storming in.

The voices started: the predictions, events that would happen over the next few weeks. "Japan at risk. A large hurricane in the Gulf of Mexico, headed for Louisiana. Volcanic activity in Australia and New Zealand."

"Stop! Stop!" she screamed. "I can't take anymore. There's nothing I can do. Everybody thinks I'm crazy."

She pulled the duvet over her head; no wonder the world rejected her. All she'd ever wanted since she'd been a child was for the voices to stop, to find a sense of belonging in the world and to be loved. She was missing out on life, she knew that, but what could she do about it? How could she break this vicious cycle?

The shock of her father's death had hit her like a punch to the stomach; a cloak of confusion, rage and disbelief had descended on her already-chaotic mind. Her mother's death, six months prior to her father's, had been easier to bear as she'd suffered so much prior to it that there had been a sense of relief around it.

Her thoughts drifted to love and relationships. She'd never dated anyone for longer than three months. It always ended in disaster, so she'd not dated for the last two years, preferring to stay clear of all the anguish it always caused her. But now she pondered what it was that she would like from a relationship. Somebody she could trust, and who was dependable, who understood her unique ways. Did that type of guy even exist?

Maybe she should just up and go. What did she have to lose? She could travel the world, getting jobs along the way. Maybe it would give her life some purpose.

No longer able to bear staying in the basement, she headed out, desperate for some fresh air and to be free of the stench of her own home. The world around her transformed as she climbed the steps upwards to civility. The leafy neighbourhood she now found herself in was a total contrast to her world below ground. The beautiful lines of trees shaded out the summer heat.

As she walked slowly along the street, she was aware that a sense of failure was eating away at her spirit. She was drowning in her own thoughts. She understood that she had the power to change, but she just didn't know how to achieve it. Where would she be in six months time, if she did nothing to make those changes now?

Inwardly, she groaned as she saw Kyla Allan walking towards her. It was too late to hide now; they were on a collision course. Kyla had been her manager at the restaurant up until a couple of months ago, when she'd left to go on to 'better things' as she'd described her reason for leaving.

Kyla was 'full of herself', believing that she was better than all of those around her, especially Alison. She lived in a big house, drove a fancy car and never stopped bragging about her life.

Chapter 2

Coughing nervously, Alison made her excuses to Kyla and practically ran along the road to escape any further conversation. Her throat felt dry and scratchy. She should have had a drink before she left her flat, but she'd been so eager to get some air she'd forgotten to have one. She felt tired and dizzy, and the pollen in the air caused her to sneeze. She hoped she wasn't getting a cold and that it was just hay fever.

She inhaled a deep breath through her nose, held it for a second and then released it from her mouth. The last thing she wanted to do was start hyperventilating in public.

Feeling calmer, she headed for the café at the top of the street hoping that there would be a seat available outside in the glorious midday sun. She was in luck, the café was quiet and she settled into a seat and ordered a cup of tea.

She studied the flowers in the plant pot

beside her: red geraniums in full bloom. The restaurant she'd always dreamed of owning would have been brimming with flowers. She would have called it 'The Flower Restaurant'. People would have travelled from all over the country, not only for the food and service, but to admire the beautiful blooms. She sipped her tea, daydreaming.

A cat rubbed against her leg causing her to jump. It darted off in chase of a squirrel before she had chance to bend down and stroke it.

Startled, Alison looked around her as everything started to feel misty. She could hear phones ringing, all at different pitches, but as always, she knew they were all a figment of her overactive mind. There were no phones around her … no phones actually ringing. They were only in her own imagination.

Her head felt as though it was full of cotton wool. What was wrong with her? Was she never going to feel normal?

Again, she went through the ritual of the breathing exercises to prevent herself from having a panic attack. She left the café as quickly as she could. She needed to walk. She didn't know where to, but she knew she had to walk. Was she really going mad? Was she as crazy as everybody believed she was? She steadied herself against a tree trunk, inhaled a few times and repeated the words, "I am normal", out loud, over and over again.

Angry and frustrated with herself, she carried on walking and was surprised to find that she had entered the restaurant where she worked. It was time to do it.

She soon found her manager and in less than two minutes she was exiting the door, having quit her job. She smiled to herself; she was taking charge of her life. The anxiety, fear and anger lifted, as she walked defiantly along the street, her head held high in the air.

She headed through the park gates towards the flowerbeds. The fragrance of the flowers always made her feel brighter, and today was no exception as she breathed in the lovely aromas of lavender, citrus and rose. They were her three favourites.

Giggling to herself, and trying to suppress a loud laugh, she felt happier than she had for a long time. She no longer had to turn up for work at that stupid restaurant.

Unable to contain it any longer, the giggling increased in strength and turned into a full-scale chuckle.

The following day, after the best night's sleep she'd had in ages, she set off on the holiday, which she'd spontaneously booked the night before. She'd dreamed of going away for a while, so she had booked herself a week away by the sea.

After checking into the bed and breakfast in Bournemouth, she headed towards the beach. Kicking off her sandals, she walked along with the sand tickling her toes. She could taste the salty seawater in her mouth, and her nose was filled with the aromatic sea air.

After cleaning the sand from her feet under the little tap at the top of the promenade and placing her sandals back on her feet, she spotted a little Italian restaurant with tables outside, laid ready for lunch. It was an old rustic building, but the waiter made her feel welcome and she chose a seat on the terrace, facing the sea. She ordered garlic bread to start but was disappointed when it arrived, as there was not enough garlic. It tasted just like plain bread. The main course of lasagne contained very little meat, and although the sauce was tasty, it didn't cover up this fact. She left, feeling rather disappointed. No restaurant of hers would provide such low quality food.

A bench was in sight, so she headed towards it. And there she sat, staring idly at the waves rolling onto the beach, whilst pondering how she was going to make ends meet after her holiday. She lit a cigarette and watched the smoke blowing casually around in the sea air. She watched as people passed and realised that her focus had turned to the men, particularly those who appeared to be single.

She stopped herself. What was she doing? Embarrassed, she stubbed out her cigarette, took a notepad and pen from her handbag and pretended to write. Somehow this made her feel less conspicuous, although she didn't understand why she felt obliged to look as though she was busy. Why couldn't she just sit still and take in the beauty of her surroundings?

Her thoughts drifted on. Her mind was certainly not her friend as she doodled pointless patterns in her notebook.

A man took a seat beside her on the bench.

"Lovely day. Mind if I join you? I'm Darren." He offered her his hand to shake.

She closed her notebook and offered her hand in return.

"Yeah, it's a lovely day," she felt her body stiffen.

"I saw you eating outside at the restaurant. I was inside. Did you enjoy your meal? Can't say mine was any good. What did you say your name was?"

"I didn't, but it's Alison. My meal wasn't great

either."

"Suppose we should stick to eating Italian food in Italy, where it belongs," he laughed.

"I've never been to Italy."

"Oh, you don't know what you're missing out on, but you're a good few years younger than me. Plenty of time for you to travel the world. Sicily! You should try Sicily. You'd love it there."

"When would be the best time to go?"

"September … or October. Would be lovely then. If you enjoy good food and fine wine, then you should definitely go."

She didn't know why, but she felt herself opening up to this stranger whom she had only just met. She felt comfortable in his presence. He made her remember how much she missed talking to her dad.

"I love food and especially wine, I'm going to open my own restaurant one day."

"A foodie then, are you?"

"Yes … but I like art and music … and flowers. I love flowers. My restaurant is going to be full of flowers. People will come from far and wide to see them."

"Sounds lovely. I'll come and eat there one

day."

He looked at his watch. "Unfortunately, I have to go but I've enjoyed chatting with you. I don't want to put you under any pressure … I realise that you're a lot younger than me … but if you'd care to join me for dinner tomorrow night, then I'll meet you at 6:30 on this same bench. I'll take you somewhere special. I'll book a table for two in hope, but please don't feel bad if you can't make it, I'll just talk to myself all night."

She watched him walk away.

Chapter 3

The following evening having met Darren on the bench at 6:30 pm, Alison now found herself sitting opposite him inside an intriguing and mysterious speakeasy.

"Isn't it great in here," he said. "It goes back to the time when alcohol was prohibited in America."

"Yeah, it's fab. I loved the hidden entrance. It feels very clandestine, Mr ... Oh! I don't know your surname."

"Marlowe ... Darren Marlowe."

"Mr Marlowe."

"They serve good food here, as well. I've booked us a table for later."

"It's swanky in here. I like it. It's exciting."

"Yes. It's sophisticated ... for a sophisticated young lady."

She sipped her cocktail.

"Thank you. I'm glad I came. I wasn't sure." She turned her head to watch the pianist playing the piano in the corner."

"It's like stepping back into the 1920s, isn't it? Come on! Let's go and find our table. You have to push the bookcase, and it will open into a small room with our own private, little dining table for two."

"Wow! It's such a hidden treasure. How did you manage to book the only remaining table with such short notice?"

As they sat and ate dinner, Alison thought about what it might be like to kiss him. She studied his face. Cute, but at least 20 years older than her. Did it matter? She wasn't sure. Surely, if she hadn't liked him, she wouldn't have turned up. And she'd spent ages getting ready, trying to look good.

She drank some more water. She mustn't drink too much of that delicious red wine he'd chosen for them to go with their mouth-watering steaks. She was pleased that she'd made an effort with her clothes, especially when he'd told her that she looked fabulous. Although, without her jacket, the strapless dress felt as though she was revealing a little too much of her body, and she was very aware that he probably knew she wasn't wearing a bra.

She felt suddenly hot as he leaned across the table towards her and gently touched the back of her hand. She couldn't help herself from flirting with him as she played with her hair, laughed and touched his arm in return.

The atmosphere was perfect, the room was fairly dark, lit only with candlelight, and she couldn't stop herself from lightly touching his shirt and feeling its softness against her fingers. She felt so nervous as she realised how much she liked him. She wanted to make a good impression. She mustn't allow herself to become self-conscious and put him off.

After the meal was finished, he asked, "Where are you staying, Alison? Can I walk you back? I presume it's in town … somewhere nearby."

As they started to walk, the rain came from nowhere, the stinging raindrops hitting them hard and soaking their clothes.

He laughed. "I'm totally unprepared for this. I've no brolly and no coat. Let's stand under the cover of this doorway, and I'll call us a taxi."

He took out his phone and did just that.

"It'll be five minutes, Alison. Can I see you

again? I've so enjoyed your company tonight."

"And I've enjoyed yours, too. Thank you so much, but you should have let me pay for my half of the dinner. I was planning on hiring a bike and going for a ride tomorrow. You can join me if you like?"

"I can do better than that. I've got two bikes, so you won't need to hire one."

She fiddled nervously with her watch as they waited for the taxi. She really did like him, and she hoped that he would at least give her a goodnight kiss. She looked up at him.

"I really have had a lovely evening. I feel so comfortable around you. I need to know though, Darren. Are you married? I need you to be honest."

She felt the atmosphere change.

"Yes, Alison. I am. But I don't love her anymore."

"You know that I'm psychic, don't you, Darren?"

"Yes, of course I do, and you already know that I am, as well," he said.

"This is going to happen whether we like it or not. We will be together in Florence in the autumn. I can see us both inside a church: Santo Spirito. I can smell the candles and the incense. I can also see two red hearts. That's us," she said.

Chapter 4

As Alison and Darren rode their bikes towards the coastal path, Darren said, "Bournemouth is a lovely place. I've lots to show you: secret passages and private gardens. We'll ride to Dragonfly Garden first; it's a lovely private park that not many people know about. It's quite a spooky place, but as far as I'm aware, there are no bodies buried there."

After five miles of bumpy coastal path, they arrived at the park. They parked their bikes against a tree and sat on a bench to take in the beauty of their surroundings. Then, after a little rest, they walked across a bridge over the pond.

Alison stopped in her tracks, "Can you hear that? It sounds like monks chanting."

"Yes … and I've just felt something touch my arm. I told you that it was spooky here."

"They've stopped chanting. They're

whispering."

"I can smell burning, but I can't see a fire anywhere."

"I always carry my infrared camera with me. I'll take a few shots ... see if I can capture any images."

She turned to Darren, and as she did so, an intrusive image of him making love to her on the bridge snapped through her mind.

A man walking by with his dog broke the thought.

Darren suggested that they head to a café just outside the park, and they sat opposite each other, him sipping his black, and Alison her cappuccino. She felt a sense of calm she hadn't felt for a long time.

"So, when did your psychic awareness start, Alison?"

"When I was a child. I still don't really understand it."

"I thought it was just heightened intuition to begin with," Darren said.

"Electrical stuff is a nightmare for me. Things switch on and off by themselves all the time."

He laughed. "It's light bulbs with me ... always blowing out."

"Batteries drain on me. My phone is forever dying."

"I feel drained a lot of the time … no energy. My wife has no understanding of any of it."

"I've never fitted in anywhere. I've never found anywhere I could really consider home."

"Do you think sex can be spiritual, Alison?"

"I'm not sure. Is it spiritual or fantasy?"

He seemed amused by her answer, and she panicked, wondering if he could see the images of them making love that were running through her head.

"I don't think sex is about the soul," he ventured.

"It depends how romantic you are, I think."

Less than two hours later, they were in Alison's hotel bedroom in the throes of passion. His breathing was fast and loud, and he called out her name as he quickened his thrusts.

Her mind was engaged. To her, it wasn't just a physical act, although her hips swung with a mind of their own, and her mouth moaned for more as he sucked and bit at her nipples. He was rougher than she'd imagined and had instantly pushed her up against the wall before she'd barely managed to close the door behind them. He had ripped off her clothes, entering her fast and furiously.

They both exploded like a volcano, the pressure having built to a tumultuous climax. Afterwards, they lay in each other's arms, silent. Their bodies spoke their own language. Their nudity had opened them up to an acute knowledge of each other. They were of one mind, one voice.

He broke the silence. "It was inevitable."

Still feeling aroused, she whispered, "Yes."

She knew that she should be honest with him and tell him about her diagnosis – that she was schizophrenic – but she didn't want to spoil everything. Not just yet anyway. Surely, she could hide her psychosis from him for a while. After all, she'd not felt suicidal for a long time now. It's not as if he was in any imminent danger from her.

Her mind was in turmoil: a foggy space. She couldn't trust her judgement; she no longer knew what was true.

She flicked her hair, pursed her lips and leant over to kiss him, allowing her armour to fall away.

Relishing in the close proximity of his naked body, she moved in closer to him, feeling excited but fragile, frail, afraid and vulnerable.

His body made her heart pound, and she could feel butterflies in her stomach … but she also felt scared. It was as if her mind and body were at war with one another. Did she need to put up a shield? How could she feel fear and desire, all at once? Unable to stop herself, she started to laugh.

A loud ringing began in her ears. Phones were ringing everywhere. She needed this to stop … now! The sound changed to whooshing ocean waves. At least this was more bearable, but then it changed again to an annoying, cricket-like chirping. Her body jumped as she then heard the screeching of brakes. She clenched her jaw, trying to make the noises go away.

Deathly still, she lay next to him, listening. There was now a presence in the room.

A growling voice in the background called, "Alison, Alison."

There was definitely an entity in their midst. She heard it laugh menacingly.

"Did you hear that?" she enquired of Darren.

"Hear what? No, I didn't hear anything."

"I think there's something demonic in here. Something malevolent."

"I don't feel anything, and anyway, I'm not convinced about the demonic side of things.

I've never met an evil spirit."

Hot and sweaty, she moved away from Darren onto the other side of the double bed. As she did so, she caught sight of four fingers around the knob on the bedroom door.

She started to panic. Looking back at Darren, his face looked strange and distorted.

Something scratched her neck.

"Don't do that, Darren. Why would you scratch me like that?"

"I didn't!"

She froze. Two black, shadowy figures danced together before her eyes.

The energy in the room had shifted.

"Darren, are you sure you didn't scratch my neck?"

"No, but I can feel that the room has suddenly gone freezing cold and that's not logical. It's a hot, sunny day."

A surging sense of power overcame her as the inner voices and inner visions emerged. She was totally engaged with the emotions and senses. Her demons were using her life energy, making her feel strange and dreamy. Voices were coming from deep inside her.

"Can you hear the voices, Darren?"

"No, but that doesn't mean you can't."

"Have you cheated on your wife before?"

"No! I've never felt a passion towards anyone else like I have towards you."

A shiver ran down Alison's spine as she gave him a look. A warning ... setting a boundary! She was establishing dominance as the energy coursed through her body.

Her brain's pleasure chemical, dopamine, was playing havoc with her.

Her phone rang! Or did it? She was too engrossed in her own thoughts to respond.

"Do you want to know all about me? Where I was born? About my childhood? Everything?"

He quietly nodded. "Yes."

"Good! I want you to get to know me ... I mean properly get to know me."

Chapter 5

After Darren had left, Alison reflected on the day that she had spent with him. Not telling him about her diagnosis – had that been the same as telling him a lie? She just hadn't wanted to spoil anything between them. A myriad of thoughts raced through her mind. She just wanted him to like her ... that was all.

She opened the window of her room and breathed in the scent of the freshly cut lawns below. It relaxed her, and she could feel a sense of joy in her heart. She took a deep breath in again and this time caught the aroma of the roses. The kettle had boiled, and she poured the boiling water into a mug containing a sachet of peppermint tea, a drink which always elevated her mood and stimulated her mind.

He hadn't asked to see her that evening but had taken her phone number and told her that he would be in touch.

A PARALLEL PERSONA

After drinking her tea, she decided to go swimming. She'd spotted the pool located not far from where she was staying when she'd first arrived. Swimming goggles placed firmly on her head, she dived in and began to swim front crawl. She was a strong swimmer, fast, with a fluent style. Her strange thoughts were always under control when she focused on her stroke.

She was no longer seeing a psychiatrist; she'd discharged herself from the hospital's services a few years previously. She was proud of herself for not needing one now. Her willpower was strong as she pushed herself to complete 50 lengths of the Olympic-sized pool. She no longer felt the need for medication. It had never helped anyway.

Rewarding herself with a spell in the Jacuzzi for having completed the lengths, a man with dreadlocks and a ready smile climbed in next to her. Initially, they did not talk to one another. Then, boom, they were suddenly talking as if they had known each other for years.

She could feel the excitement ramping up in her as he asked, "Have you eaten? Would it be too late for me to take you out for dinner?"

"Sounds great," she heard herself reply.

"We'd best get out of here and get ready then. Where did you say you were staying? Can I meet you there ... at 8:30? Is that long enough for you to get ready?"

Climbing out of the Jacuzzi, she smiled back at him.

"I'll be ready, Antony."

"Great! See you shortly."

The rain had started to bucket down as she raced back to the bed and breakfast to get ready, overexcited at the thought of dinner with this guy. After, taking a shower, she poured herself a glass of Chardonnay from the complimentary bottle, which had been placed in her room, and started to blow-dry her hair.

As she walked into the reception area at 8:35, Antony was sitting in an armchair waiting for her. He linked arms with her as they stepped outside, the rain having given way to a pleasant evening.

He smiled at her. "You had me at hello, you know. You're very beautiful. I feel honoured to have you on my arm."

He bent down and kissed her on her cheek. She felt her insides melt. She already craved for more. Her emotional system was running amok when, for the first time since meeting Antony, she remembered Darren, which made her feel miserable and sad. Why did she feel a sense of loss around him? She hadn't lost him;

he'd said that he would call her. He didn't need to know about Antony, and anyway, he had a wife. Why was her life always in a stew?

"I've managed to get us a booking for dinner on a sunset cruise. I thought you'd like that."

Alison's head started to spin. She felt disorientated and dizzy. She tripped and Antony steadied her.

"Are you okay?"

Eager to seem fine, she muttered, "Yes, I just tripped."

She was finding it difficult to concentrate as the ringing phones started in her ears. Everything felt as though it was spinning out of control. *Damn the unpredictability of this illness,* she thought to herself.

Trying to focus, she took in her surroundings as they walked. As they crossed the street, she watched as young children frolicked under a sprinkler in a playground. They continued into the park and took the main path towards the Cloisters, and then came out onto the coastal path where she'd been with Darren earlier that morning. This memory jolted through her as she realised that this was the second man she'd spent romantic time with in the same day.

They took the decline towards the harbour. Lush areas of green, and stone archways. *Yes,* she thought, *Bournemouth is beautiful.*

They passed a man walking his dog who acknowledged them with a nod of his head. Under a tree, a group of people were copying the moves of a man teaching them Tai Chi. An elderly couple sat on a bench, watching and looking bemused. A steep flight of steps led down to the harbour. She felt safe again, grounded, as they crossed the busy road.

They boarded the boat and entered the quiet restaurant, which looked more expensive than it probably was. Her expectations were raised as she noted it was decorated like a stylish country home. A few tourists were taking photographs. What she liked the most as she looked around were the plants ... lots of them. The hostess was friendly as she escorted them to their window-seat table. It felt classy – low-key and highly charming – a bit like her date.

The man from the next table stood up and offered Antony his hand.

"I thought it was you. How are you? Haven't seen you in a while."

"Oh, hi," he replied. "No, I've been out of the country – all work and no play. This is my friend, Alison."

The man shook her hand, exchanged pleasantries and retired to his own table to sit with a very glamorous woman, who looked half his age. Alison pondered whether that was what people had thought about her when she'd been with Darren.

The menus arrived, and there was a pretty good choice of food. As she peered over the top of her menu, she wasn't surprised to see Antony's friend practically devouring the lady he was with.

As they started to cruise, a cool, but pleasant, breeze entered the restaurant from the open doors, and it was lovely to look out of the window as they sailed out to sea.

A phone rang. At first Alison thought it was the usual annoying ringing in her ears, but then realised it was real, and it was coming from her handbag. She snatched it up and quickly pressed decline as Darren's name flashed across the screen. She recalled that he had saved his number on her phone shortly before he'd left, saying that, as he was married, it was best that he called her, but at least she'd have his number in case of an emergency.

Antony joked. "Boyfriend calling?"

She laughed. "No, he's a married friend of mine. Will you excuse me? I need the loo."

Overcome with guilt, she dashed off to the toilets and dialled Darren's number.

Should she tell him that she was out on a date?

He was pleased that she'd called him back.

"So glad you called. My wife's gone out. Do you want me to come over?"

"No, I'm sorry. I'm not available. I'm already out."

"Well, I could come and find you. Don't want you feeling lonely."

"As I already said, I'm not available. Call me tomorrow," she replied, quickly ending the conversation.

Back at the table, she ordered chicken noodle soup for her starter and a beef and barley stew for her main.

Antony smiled across the table. "I'm going to a ball on Saturday evening. I'd love you to come with me."

"I'd love to. I've never been to a ball, but I've nothing to wear."

"That's fine. If you're free tomorrow, we'll go shopping and choose you something."

"How lovely! Yes, please." She beamed at him.

Was this love at first sight, she thought? She had an overwhelming feeling that it may be. She locked eyes with him and smiled again. It was as if she'd known him before in another life. Was he going to be the one?

His scent drifted across the table, a combination of his body odour, musk and deodorant. Bright-coloured auras shone around him. Dressed in a Ralph Lauren shirt and a smart suit, his quirky style attracted her, being totally at odds with his dreadlocks. His dark olive skin added to his air of mystery. Alison wondered about his childhood. He'd already told her that he'd grown up in New York and that his father had been a church minister. She also knew that Antony had a mischievous sense of humour and he was extremely self-confident. As she observed him, she experienced butterflies in her stomach. How could she feel this way about two different men at the same time? Was it immoral?

"Have you travelled much, Alison?"

"No, barely at all," she replied.

He leant across the table and held her hand. "Well, I will have to put that to rights and show you the world."

She didn't know how to answer that, so she remained silent. He obviously had no idea how screwed up her mind was. She felt guilty as she thought back over her day. Stifling a nervous cough, she placed her hand in front of her mouth. He was talking, but she wasn't listening to what he was saying as her thoughts raced away.

"I'd love to just hold you tonight."

His comment snapped her back into reality. She smiled in return.

"I have to admit, I find your dreadlocks very sexy."

"Well, I think you're very hot."

She lightly touched his arm with one hand and played with her long hair with the other as she tilted her head and gave him a beguiling pout, unaware of how childlike she appeared to be. She caught his eyes drifting down to her boobs and hovering there a little longer than he probably realised they had. Her low-cut dress and push-up bra emphasized her ample cleavage. The deep, smooth tone of his voice was turning her on, as was his athletic body.

Their starters arrived, and Alison noted how slowly he ate, as though he was appreciating every mouthful. She also observed how he constantly checked his phone, which he had placed on the table in front of him.

Something was so damned attractive about him – his effortless style, his hair which made such a statement – and she craved to learn more about him. He was unique, creative and stylish. She wished that her own clothes were a little bit more out-of-the-ordinary.

Guilt about Darren drifted over her again. She was acting badly … two men in one day. But was it irrational and inappropriate? After all, Darren was a married man, or did that just make things worse?

She'd made a mistake. That was all it was. It was just regret that she was feeling. She tried to convince herself that she'd done nothing wrong. After all, nobody was perfect, were they? But an intense feeling of fear and dread overcame her.

Studying him, she watched him rub his right eyebrow with his index finger from end to end along the entire length of his brow. It happened in a flash. She wished she didn't see things in such detail, so she briefly shut her eyes and turned her head to look away.

It was as if, since meeting Antony, her heart had grown bigger by ten sizes. He smiled at her, and she smiled back. And there it was again. That stupid thing she'd done earlier with Darren: she started to laugh.

His reaction took her by surprise as he grinned at her. The restaurant no longer existed. It was as though it was just the two of them.

"I'm schizophrenic," she blurted out. This was something she had never admitted voluntarily to anyone before. It was as if some cosmic force had made her say it.

Antony's knife slid out of his hand and hit the floor with a clank. Alison laughed even louder, although she felt as if she was dying on the inside. The fear coursed through her body as her world started to close in.

"It's alright, Alison. I'm so sorry. My timing was completely off. I didn't drop my knife as a reaction to what you said. It just slipped from my hand. I really don't care if you're schizophrenic. I appreciate your honesty."

She felt nothing. She didn't respond.

"Are you angry with me? Say something."

Closing her eyes, a single tear ran down her cheek.

"I haven't told anybody that since I was 16. Do you think I'm mad?"

He reached over and held her fingers, intertwining them with his own as she blinked back any potential further tears. Her laughing had subsided to giggles.

He looked her in the eye. "I have complete

sympathy for you. It must be an awful condition to have to live with."

Her right hand cramped, and she removed it from his grasp. Four of her fingers curled inwards in agony.

"Have you ever met anyone like me?"

"Relax, Alison. I'm not out to hurt you."

Raising her eyebrows, she met his eyes with her own.

"I don't want to do anything that I'll regret."

He looked at her, puzzled by her remark.

"What do you mean?"

"Can you walk me back to my guest house, please?"

"I can, but there's no reason to retreat. I'm enjoying your company."

Alison stared at her hands, her fingers having now relaxed.

"You do think I'm mad, don't you?"

"Of course not! I think you're lovely, and utterly charming."

She found his words difficult to believe. Her mood had changed completely, and she began to feel angry and upset.

"Well, I don't fucking well believe you.

Everyone thinks I'm mad."

"You're just feeling delicate, that's all, because you've shown me how vulnerable you are."

Her rage quickly subsided.

"I'm sorry! I didn't mean to swear."

"And I'm sorry that you're finding this so difficult to talk about."

Antony paid the bill, and they left the boat, which had harboured thirty minutes before. He held her hand as they walked back towards the guesthouse.

"I'd still like to take you shopping tomorrow, Alison."

"I'd like to go, but I know myself well enough to admit that I can't be trusted. I don't want to hurt you."

"I'm not afraid of your diagnosis. It doesn't scare me."

"I change so quickly … my moods … you would never cope with me."

A silence fell between them as they walked along.

He broke the silence.

"It's just a label. That's all it is."

"But it's not though, is it? I hear voices all the time. Voices from spirit! I know things I shouldn't know. Things that are going to happen before they do."

Chapter 6

The following day, Alison felt as if she needed to try and take some control over her life.

She texted Darren. *'If you loved me, you would tell your wife about me.'*

She then texted Antony. *'I'll go shopping with you to get that ball gown for Saturday night, but only if you agree that this has to be an open relationship. I can't do monogamous, not yet anyway.'*

As soon as she had sent them, she started to wonder if it had been a bad idea, and she shouted aloud, "No! We are not going down that road again."

The monsters in her head were driving her crazy.

Her phone 'pinged'. It was a reply from Darren. *'I'm sorry, Alison, I will tell her soon. But my wife is unwell at the moment. It's not the right time.'*

Another 'ping', this time from Antony. *'That's*

fine by me. I'll come over to your place at 11. We'll have fun choosing you a dress.'

Relieved that they'd both responded so quickly, her choice was now easier. She would give Darren the silent treatment if he called, and she'd focus her attention on Antony.

Despite this, her thoughts drifted back to Darren. He wasn't going to get away with this so easily. She was magnetically drawn to him; he would be hers one day. But did he not know that she had incredibly deep feelings for him? How dare he make her feel so insecure? It had all felt so romantic with him yesterday. She'd found him to be fascinating. How dare he cause her pain like this?

She wanted his attention now. She could feel herself working up into some type of rage. How dare he reject her like this? They had experienced such a strong passion. He would not remain unobtainable to her. He had been deceitful, and she hated deceit. They were supposed to be travelling to Italy together one day, weren't they?

She checked her watch; it was already 10 o'clock. She had an hour to get ready to meet Antony.

Firstly, she needed to exercise. She lay on her back on the floor, with her knees bent. Then she placed her palms on the top of her hips and proceeded to do 20 opposite arm and leg lifts. Afterwards, she performed 20 squats, pressing her hands gently into her sides.

Feeling lifted by her efforts, Alison jumped into the shower. The hallucinations started, but she managed to keep them at bay, focusing on what type of dress she would choose for the ball.

The visions surfaced again as she watched Darren trip on a tree branch. Or had she pushed him? She wasn't sure. The hamster in her head was starting to race on its wheel, and she began to weep. Trying to distract her thoughts, she started to count backwards from a hundred and think about the lovely day that she was about to spend with Antony.

She glanced at her watch; it had just turned 11. She put the finishing touch to her look by fixing a pair of silver, boho hoop earrings into her ear lobes. She was now ready.

He greeted her with a smile and a kiss on her cheek.

"You look beautiful, Alison. We can walk into town to look for a dress for you, if that's what you'd like to do?"

"That'd be great. Thank you," she said, wondering if she'd overdone her look with the orange lipstick, navy-blue eyeliner and pale-blue eye shadow.

As they walked towards the town centre, she couldn't stop herself from occasionally glancing over at Antony; she really did find him attractive. She wanted his lips to kiss hers. She reached for his hand and interlocked her fingers around his. A wave of happiness and pleasure raced through her as he squeezed her hand.

"What sort of dress do you think I should buy for the ball?"

"A long one … classy and sexy."

Her mind switched to her finances. How was she going to pay for this? She'd given up her job and hadn't paid the rent on her flat or the bills for that month, although she did have a little nest egg, which her father had left her, sitting in the bank. She would have to break into it.

She suddenly realised that she had no intention of ever going back to her flat. She was going to start her life over, so she didn't need to worry about her rent. Her landlord would never find her, and anyway, it was time for her to move on from that depressing, dingy place.

There! It was decided. She was never going back, and she would find part-time work to top up the money her father had left her. She had her passport and birth certificate with her. What more did she need?

A smile crossed her face, and the sunlight lit her day. She was free. It was time to have some fun.

They entered the first shop that Antony had suggested, and Alison ran her fingers across the textures of all the different fabrics. She was astounded at the choice of colours. She was excited and happy.

Alison reached up to Antony and gave him a spontaneous kiss on his cheek as a strong feeling of gratitude overcame her.

"Just being with you makes me feel happy, Alison."

"I'd like you to choose my dress for me. There's so much choice. I've no idea which one would suit me best."

Antony grinned, "What am I going to do with you? Don't worry, you'd look great in any of them."

"I don't want anything too expensive; my purse won't stretch to it."

She was shocked at his reply.

"Don't worry! I'm buying it for you."

A PARALLEL PERSONA

Fluttering around the shop, knowing that she no longer needed to be scared of the price tags, the dresses took on an even greater appeal. They were all gorgeous. She felt as though she was six years old again, standing in her favourite sweet shop, choosing from the vast array of goodies, but never being able to make a decision on which ones she really wanted, because she actually wanted them all.

"There are loads of lovely ones. Please help me to choose. I just don't know."

She turned to Antony.

"Well, let's find this dream ball gown together, then."

He led her around the shop, studying the gowns on the rails. He pulled out a powder blue one, edged with exquisite detail.

"I'm so grateful to you for this. Should I try this one on?" She glanced at the price tag; she could never have afforded anything like this.

"Yes, of course! Try it on!" He handed it to her.

Alison smiled, her heart pounding in her chest. She hesitated at the entrance to the changing room, as the shop assistant took the gown from her and led her in,

"Such a beautiful dress! Step this way, please.

If you need any help with the zip, just call me."

Staring at herself in the full-length mirror, adorned in the expensive dress, she smiled and mouthed quietly, "You deserve this. This is how your life should be."

She carried on staring at her image in the mirror. She looked like a princess. She felt light-headed with happiness. A man who was prepared to spend this much money on her after just one date! She couldn't believe it. It was as though she was in some type of wonderful dream.

All of a sudden, the cubicle felt hot and airless, so she clambered out of the dress and put her jeans and lightweight jumper back on. Falling in love with Antony was going to be easy, but how would he cope with living with a family of characters like her?

Antony's eyed lingered on her as she came out of the dressing room, Oh dear! Didn't you like it?'

"I loved it."

"Why didn't you show me, then?"

"Well, I know you've already seen it, but you haven't seen me wearing it. I want it to be a surprise."

He placed his hand in the small of her back,

and they followed the shop assistant to the counter for him to pay.

Chapter 7

It was the night of the ball. Darren had messaged a couple of times, but Alison had ignored him. She was ready 15 minutes earlier than she needed to be, and as she sat on the bed waiting, the mental imagery started, perfectly distinct and full of colour.

She was beyond excited at the thought of going to the ball with Antony, and the short time before he was due to pick her up seemed to be taking an eternity to pass. She tried to force the images away. She needed to stay alert to what was actually happening. She was determined to enjoy the night and not allow her stupid brain to spoil the evening.

They drove down an ancient, tree-lined avenue to approach the venue for the ball. Antony had collected her in a taxi so that he'd be able to have a drink without worrying about having to drive home.

A PARALLEL PERSONA

As they entered the beautiful hotel, the reception area reminded Alison of elegant, bygone days. The colours were rich, and the curtains were a plush velvet. The waiter handed them both a welcoming glass of champagne.

"I could do with a cigarette. Is there a balcony or somewhere I can have a smoke?" Alison asked.

"I'll come with you. I think there's one just through the door to the left," Antony replied.

The balcony was positioned above the hotel's swimming pool. Alison didn't know why, but she felt as though everyone else on the balcony was staring at her.

A magician approached her with a coin, which he concealed in his hand, and after a magical gesture, it mysteriously disappeared, reappearing behind her ear. She'd always loved magic and was captivated as she tried to focus on his moves. She tried hard not to allow him to distract her, so that she could work out how he was performing his tricks, but it was impossible. She relaxed and felt less uncomfortable in her surroundings, intrigued by this man.

Feeling more confident, she smiled at the strangers around her on the balcony; she was beginning to enjoy herself. She took a canapé and another glass of champagne from the waiter, thanking him. She noticed that people were actually smiling back at her, people whom she would not have generally felt comfortable around.

They were a particularly good-looking crowd, calm and positive, obviously used to this type of lifestyle. They all appeared to be a similar age to herself, the 30 to 40 bracket she would guess. A feeling of joy touched her soul. She was 'fitting in'. A sparkle of happiness was growing inside her. She looked at Antony. Was he feeling the same? A realisation that she could be more open and friendly, less fearful of people, overcame her.

Placing a hand on Antony's chest, she beamed at him.

"Shall we go inside and find our table?" Antony suggested.

"Yes," she replied. Having decided that she was going to 'rise to the occasion', she wasn't going to let him down.

Alison found herself seated between Antony and a politician from Stafford, who introduced himself as Mark Holmes, and who happily told her about his importance on the world stage. He was a large man with an equally large personality, and she found him interesting to talk with about the medical and social needs of – as he described them – the working class. He dominated the conversation but she managed to hold her own on points that she understood. Antony threw a protective arm around her shoulders and enquired if she was feeling okay.

The ringing in her ears started, but she was not going to allow it to ruin the evening; she was having such a good time. She wished that she could just make the noises stop.

She liked this man, Mark. His conversation was engaging, and although a lot of the subjects he was discussing were serious, there was also a playful tone to his voice. She estimated him to be around five years older than her. She smiled at Antony. She couldn't be having a crush on Mark, could she? What was she doing?

Her phone rang, and she snatched it from her clutch bag. Darren's name scrolled across the screen. Did she really care about Darren? She had no idea. It was all becoming so confusing. She typed out a text, *'Sorry, can't speak at the moment but I'm thinking about you.'* She pressed 'send'.

Antony leant into her and gave her a kiss on her cheek. "You really do look beautiful. I'm so glad I asked you to come."

It was a simple compliment, but the pleasure of his words coursed through her. She squeezed his hand in return. She felt good about herself, which was a rare feeling for her. She felt honoured to be in such lavish surroundings, at this sumptuous ball. She felt truly happy.

As she glanced up, she caught Mark's eyes resting longer than they should have done on the small sliver of shoulder that her dress revealed. Instinctively, she sat back in her seat, unaware of the effect that her silky skin was having on Mark, and how sexy he was finding her.

The woman who was sitting next to Mark, whom he had simply introduced as Janet, was annoying Alison for no good reason other than the fact that he had brought her along with him to the ball. He hadn't said what her relationship was to him, but he had definitely not stated that she was his wife, nor even girlfriend.

Continuing to chat with Mark, she was finding it increasingly difficult to hide her admiration for him; in fact, he was blowing her mind. He really was quite extraordinary compared to anyone else that she'd ever encountered in her life before.

It dawned on her that she really didn't know men, and that something had awakened inside her, willing her to find out more about them. She was beginning to realise that they all came in different guises, and they weren't all just the same, as she'd previously believed. Released by the death of her parents, it was now apparent to Alison that she had always tried to walk the path that they had encouraged her to do, and that now she was beginning to walk her own path. Due to her diagnosis, they had preferred her to spend time alone, or just with them. They had been masters at teaching her rejection by others, fearful that she wouldn't 'fit in'. All she had longed for was approval and acceptance, having been told constantly by them that she was different. They had made her life uncomfortable, tiring and confusing.

From today, she would listen only to her heart's desire. She would become the person that she was destined to be. Allowing herself to show her vulnerability had somehow released her. A great feeling of excitement and joy overcame her. She was no longer finding it daunting speaking to men, although she was aware that she didn't seem to be finding it so easy to make friends with people of her own gender. But she'd begun to open up; she just needed to do more. Antony had proved to her that not everyone would judge her condition negatively. She was no longer feeling awkward.

It was a moment of sudden discovery, that men actually found her attractive and that she had the capability to lure them in. She had the ability to play them. She finally felt connected. It was possible for her to live her dream. Her parents had set her in a trap, and she had allowed them to do so. It was a sad and difficult truth to face. They had never approved of her ways, nor understood her illness. She was free. She no longer had to please them, nor anyone else for that matter, just herself. She could create whatever she desired. Her illness meant that she'd never met her parents' expectations. She could see now that they'd let her down. Fear was no longer going to run her life, if only she could learn to control the various sensations in her body.

Alison sipped her white wine the waiter had poured for her. She'd refused the offer of water … probably not the wisest of moves.

Realising that she was gazing adoringly at Mark, she quickly turned her attention to Antony and gave him what she hoped he would consider her 'bedroom eyes'.

Antony excused himself from the table, and whispered to Alison, "I'll be as quick as I can. Nature calls."

Mark turned to her. "So, you and Antony … you're just friends?"

After a few seconds, she replied, "Well, we're not in a relationship, as such."

He pushed her further. "So, it's just casual then, is it?"

"Yes, it's just a bit of fun." She was aware that she was misleading him but was unable to stop herself.

This whole love thing wasn't proving to be all smooth sailing. Alison was becoming more confused by the minute. How was she feeling instant attraction to three men all at the same time? She liked them all, but in different ways. What was it she really wanted from them? Why did it all feel so tricky? She steadied herself; the alcohol was beginning to make her feel quite giddy. What did she even know about Antony? What did he even do for a living?

Mark broke her thoughts. "Not the settling down type that Antony. Never in the UK for a start, and even when he is, I've never seen him with the same woman twice. Watch out that he doesn't use you."

Fear and vulnerability flashed across Alison's face beneath her false smile that greeted his words. His words had stung her. The thought of Antony with another woman, or a string of them as Mark had implied, aroused in her the same feelings of jealousy that she felt towards

Darren's wife, and also the woman sitting next to Mark, even though he hadn't paid her much attention so far that evening.

As Antony returned to the table, panic had begun to take over her mind.

She whispered in his ear, "I don't know whether I can trust you. I don't know if I can live like this."

Antony suggested they go outside to the balcony to smoke and have a chat. She followed him, relieved that she didn't have to talk any further with Mark.

"What on earth's the matter with you? You were the one who said that you couldn't cope with a monogamous relationship; now this thing about trust springs up out of nowhere," Antony declared.

"You're not the only man interested in me, you know."

"I'm sure I'm not. You're a stunning woman. I'm sure you get a lot of attention. Mark's not been able to take his eyes off you all evening."

"I'm sorry. I was going into a rant. It happens to me all of the time. When I get scared, I become totally irrational."

"C'mon! Stay positive. We've had a lovely evening until now. Mark isn't the only man wishing that he could get inside that dress of yours. I don't know what he said to you whilst I was away from the table, but ignore it. It's not important."

"He said you have a string of women."

"To be truthful, I have had quite a few affairs, but that's all they've ever been. I've never found anyone that intrigued me, or interested me, enough to date more than a few times."

"I'm sorry! I made a mistake. I shouldn't have let him get to me like that."

"I travel a lot and I'm often away from home. But that doesn't mean that when I find the right person I wouldn't be able to stay loyal to them. It just hasn't happened yet."

"I'm glad we've had this chat. That's what I like about you. You listen to me, and you understand, even when everything that comes out of my mouth comes out all jumbled up."

"Do you want to leave? We don't have to stay if you don't want to."

"No. Let's stay. I'm not going to allow Mark to make me feel like a victim. I was enjoying myself until his last comments."

"That's my girl! Take back the power from him."

As they returned to their seats, Antony

reached across for her hand which she'd placed on the table in front of her and squeezed it. She was back on solid ground.

She squeezed his hand back in return.

"I didn't tell you how great you look in your tux."

"And I should tell you that you are driving me crazy with desire in that dress. You're making me want to do extraordinary things to you, to discover every little bit of you," he whispered in her ear.

Tears sprung into her eyes. She blinked them away, feeling guilty about how flirtatious she had been with Mark, right underneath Antony's nose. Where was her dignity and grace? She resolved herself to focus purely on Antony.

Was it normal to suddenly find herself imagining what it would be like to sleep with him? Why was her mind so set on having sex? It was as though she was having some type of sexual awakening.

He flashed her his natural, killer smile, and she melted even more.

Turning to Mark, he said, "Alison is amazing, isn't she? She doesn't know it yet, but I'm planning on making her my permanent girlfriend, if she'll have me."

A PARALLEL PERSONA

Taking her by the hand, he led her to the dance floor before Mark had even had time to register Antony's words. As he spun her around the dance floor, she couldn't remember a feeling of having so much fun. It was as though he was stealing her heart.

Chapter 8

The following evening Alison dined alone at a large pub close to her B&B, telling herself that she did not need men to create the life she wanted. She ordered a pint of cider and opened her book, although in truth she was more interested in trying to listen in to the conversation of the couple on the next table to hers, whose voices were so loud, it wasn't making the task a difficult one.

She glanced around the room. A few men were also dining solo. She checked herself. She didn't need a man.

The salmon she had ordered arrived promptly. It was delicious, but was just a small portion, and all too soon she had cleared her plate. The couple on the next table were getting romantic, clutching hands and staring into each other's eyes. Why wasn't this dating thing as plain sailing for her? She felt suddenly self-aware and awkward. She paid the bill and left as quickly as she could. Glancing at her watch, she realised that it was still only 7 o'clock. She couldn't face sitting in her empty room all evening, so she headed for the nearest bar, took a stool at the counter and ordered a large glass of wine.

Dressed in the flared, denim dress she'd treated herself to at the charity shop earlier that day, she crossed and uncrossed her legs. She thought the dress both charming and flattering. She sipped her wine, confidently. After the previous night she'd decided to play it cool with both Antony and Darren. Antony had dropped her back in a taxi, given her a perfunctory goodnight kiss and then left without even arranging a further date. She'd gone to bed furious, even though she'd had such a lovely evening. They'd both sent her texts, which she'd replied to, but she had not encouraged either of them. She intended to make the minimum effort possible.

Why couldn't she trust her own brain? Nothing ever seemed real.

Determined to try and make a female friend, she looked around her. She no longer wanted to be the person with no friends. It troubled her. What did she always do wrong? Maybe it was because she'd been the only child of elderly parents, and of course, there was her illness. But to a real friend, would any of that actually matter?

A tall, sturdy woman sat alone, further along the bar. Alison approached her.

"I hope you don't think I'm being rude, but I wondered if I could join you? I'm on my own, you see, and I could do with some company."

The woman appeared to be overjoyed at Alison's suggestion.

"Sure! Of course, I don't mind. I could do with some company myself."

An hour later, Alison was bitterly regretting speaking to the woman, whom she found vain and obnoxious. All she wanted to do was talk about herself, and she was boring. Alison made her excuses and left the bar.

Frustrated by her attempts at real life friendships, Alison headed back to the safety of her bedroom at the B&B and opened her laptop. Maybe an internet chat room would be a better option.

She was soon chatting with a 26-year-old woman from Manchester. Within half an hour, she had struck up conversation with another five women, one of whom she found extremely interesting, as she'd told her that she was a British secret agent named Mary. She explained to Alison how discreet she had to be about what she did, but as Alison began to gain her trust, she told her about their strategy and tactics for the tracking of Soviet submarines. She was unable to discuss it in detail, but Alison was impressed by the importance of her work. What she was describing seemed like science fiction, and Alison was fascinated. She described how Britain was in the process of building new attack submarines and even missile boats. Apparently, Spain was contemplating invading Gibraltar at any given moment. She had an ongoing mission of her own, but was unable to divulge any information about it, as it was top secret, other than the fact that it involved her travelling to six different countries. She warned Alison about smartphones, and how she was able to listen into any conversation, she so desired. As a spy, she was able to disappear and go off grid for weeks, or even months, on potential enemy soil, due to her highly trained skills and talents. Obviously, it was all a great risk, but she owed it to her country. Alison thought the whole idea extremely romantic and was awestruck that Mary trusted her enough to communicate with her.

'It is a little bit dangerous, you chatting on here with me, Alison. Are you sure you're okay with that, only I really need a friend I can trust?'

'Yeah. Sure, I'm okay with it. I'm finding it all quite exciting, to be honest.'

'It's critical, that you don't discuss this with anyone, and also, if you could delete the chat when we've finished.'

Alison's phone buzzed. A text from Darren, *'Missing you! Can we meet up tomorrow?'*

Feeling a lot more positive after her chat with Mary, she replied, *'Sure! What shall we do, and what time shall I meet you?'*

'Great! I'm so pleased you've agreed to meet. I thought we could do a museum, an early dinner and then maybe a movie?'

The following morning, Darren held her hand as they walked towards the museum.

"My wife's out of town for a few days ... gone to stay with her sister."

Looking up at his face, she still fancied him. But it bothered her that he hadn't told his wife that their marriage was over. She felt herself bristle at the thought and promptly removed her hand from his.

"When are you going to tell her that it's over?"

"Soon, Alison. Very soon. I promise."

The small museum was hosting an exhibition

on the history of fashion.

The Georgian era had always interested her, and she found it to be no exception at the museum. She loved learning about eye miniatures, or lovers' eyes. They had been the height of fashion, a portrait of their lover's eyes worn on rings, brooches and pendants.

The woman came from nowhere, all guns blazing, screaming and shouting at Darren, before slapping Alison sharply across the face.

Alison lunged at her. With no control over her actions, she pinned her to the wall, her fingers digging deeply into the front of her throat. Darren tried to pull Alison off, but the woman slumped to the floor, desperately fighting for air.

Darren's words rang in Alison's ears.

"It didn't mean anything, love. She means nothing to me."

She grimaced as she tightened her fingers around the woman's throat. She was five years old again, and it was herself choking and spluttering for air as her mother washed her hair, forcing her head under the bath tap so firmly that she couldn't breathe. Well, now *she* had the power and the control. Not her mother.

At that moment she hated this woman —

Darren's wife – and her own mother with every fibre of her being. They had become one, ruining her life, spoiling her relationships: her mother who prevented her from having any friends; and now this woman, with Darren.

His hands finally managed to pull Alison away from his wife, and he unceremoniously shoved her against one of the fashion dummies, which crashed to the floor, Alison straddled over the top. Realisation of what she had just done hit home as she looked over at the woman, who was now fighting for her life.

Time slowed, and everything seemed to be happening in slow motion. Alison's mother appeared in front of her, shaking her head and wagging her finger. The phones started ringing from all directions around the room. Angels appeared around the woman. She watched as Darren held the woman's head in his lap, stroking her hair away from her face. Tears rolled down Alison's cheeks. She wanted him to be holding her, not this woman … not his wife. Alison's head throbbed. She blinked. Was this real, or was it a nightmare?

Paramedics arrived. The woman was unconscious.

Darren was now her enemy. She remembered his words: "It didn't mean anything, love. She means nothing to me."

A PARALLEL PERSONA

She struggled with the security guard as he roughly handed her over to the police. Her head was spinning. She wanted to vomit. She wanted to die.

The policeman pushed her into the backseat of the police car. She threw her head back into the headrest and sobbed. She was five years old again … vulnerable and terrified. The dream of opening her 'flower restaurant' slipped further and further away as the gravity of the situation dawned on her. The clouds of her mind drifted in, the shadows becoming darker, swallowing her. Why couldn't her life just be normal? She closed her eyes, and tried to shut everything out.

A male police officer sat opposite her across the table in the same type of green plastic chair as herself.

"So, tell me what happened," he started.

"Well, Darren – the husband – has been messing around."

"From where I sit, you are looking at a charge of attempted murder, and that's only if she makes it," he continued.

"He just went insane … tried to kill her," she lied.

"You can't try and pin this on him. We know you attacked her. You need to confess your guilt if you want a lighter sentence."

"She let him down, you see. Told him she'd gone to her sister's and then just turned up at the museum, attacking us both. She's to blame, really. She attacked him first and then me. I think he just lost it."

"The woman's fighting for her life. You need to tell us the truth."

"She's been violent towards him before. He told me. He doesn't love her. He loves me."

"So, you knew that he was a married man, but you continued to have an affair?"

"I fell in love. It's as simple as that."

"Do you have mental health issues, Alison?" the officer asked.

"I'm insane, yes. That doesn't make me attack somebody to the point of near death."

"So, are you trying to tell me that you are the innocent victim in all of this?"

"It's complicated. My mental health issues, I mean."

"What's your diagnosis, Alison?"

"I'm a victim of my parents' abuse."

"Have you ever tried to commit suicide?"

"Yes. I live my life in a state of perpetual

distress."

"So, you lost your temper and tried to kill her?"

"I'm crazy, but I wouldn't do that."

"You felt betrayed, right? You went into a rage, right?"

"This is a set up. I was talking to a woman from British Intelligence last night. Is that what this is about? Is it because she told me stuff I shouldn't know?"

"I think we need to get you evaluated by a doctor, Alison. I'll make the arrangements."

Alison was taken to a secure psychiatric care facility to be assessed, where her condition worsened.

"Why is everybody spying on me?" She questioned anyone who came into contact with her. "They are watching me! Why is everybody watching me?"

The staff tried to reassure her that everything was okay and that she was safe.

"Where's Darren? Where's Antony?" she questioned them. "Why am I being held captive in this cage?"

She tried to open the security-locked door, pressing the buzzer endlessly. Giving up, she entered the communal area where a couple of other residents were watching television. They didn't seem surprised at her presence. In fact, they ignored her. But before she knew it, she had started a heated argument with one of the women.

The lights in this place were driving her insane. Why did they all have halos around them? Why was it all so dim and dark? The images started in her head once more.

The female psychiatrist sat across the table from her.

"What's troubling you, Alison?"

"The halos around the lights. I can't stand them."

"What can I do to help you?"

"You can stop treating me like a rat in an experimental lab, and let me out of here."

"I think we have some issues to deal with before we can contemplate doing that, Alison. We need to work together on this."

"My brain just doesn't think right."

"So we need to address that way of thinking. Tell me about your childhood."

"It was sad."

"Our childhood affects us, but we shouldn't

allow it to define us."

"So, what can I do to help myself?"

"Firstly, you have to come to terms with your past through therapy."

"I'm not mental. Everyone thinks I'm crazy."

"I don't think you're crazy. I think you just need help."

"I don't want to take medication. It doesn't help. I took it for years."

"Maybe it was the wrong type of medication. We can explore that."

"I get so angry."

"The medication I prescribe will help with that."

"I can't make or maintain friends."

"That's just because you've never learned how to."

"The voices and the images won't leave me alone."

"We can find a way of helping you with that."

Sleep came quickly after the psychiatrist had given her the new medication. She twitched in her bed as the dreams rolled in.

Chapter 9

Alison woke up feeling strange. She had no idea where she was. Everything felt surreal. She was clearly in some type of institution, but how and why was she here?

This surely wasn't right. She was alarmed. She needed to think straight. How long had she been here? She didn't feel safe. Where was her phone? Who had betrayed her? Who had put her here? This was immoral. Why was her thinking so distorted? She had rights, didn't she? She felt terrified. She shuddered as a chill ran down her spine. Why was she being punished? She needed to find somebody. She had so many questions to ask to sort out this nightmare. Was she in danger? Where was her freedom? This whole situation was awful and completely unbearable. This couldn't be real. She must be dreaming.

A lady in a white coat entered her room.

"Hello, I'm Dr. Horne. I'm pleased to meet you, Alison."

"What type of doctor, are you?"

"I'm a psychiatrist. I'm interested in learning all about you."

"There's no mystery about me. I'm just plain old Alison Ware."

"Well, I'm sure there's a lot more about you than just that."

"Why am I here?"

"For us to help you, Alison."

"What football team do you support?" Alison asked.

"I don't really support a team. What about you?"

"What about rugby? Do you follow rugby?"

Dr. Horne smiled. "I'm not a rugby fan either, I'm afraid."

Alison smiled back. "I don't like football or rugby. I was just testing you."

"It's okay. You're allowed to test me." She smiled again.

"Do you think I'm weird?" Alison laughed.

"Not weird, Alison … just a little different."

"What do you want from me?"

"I want to get to know you ... to try and understand you, so that we can give you the help that you need."

"If I tell you the truth, you won't want to know me."

"Try me. You've nothing to lose."

"I don't know if I can trust you."

"Of course you don't, but I know you can."

"I'm not so sure."

"There's no hurry, Alison. It's on your terms. Only when you're ready."

"Do you think that when men have affairs they are just motivated by sex?"

"I think studies show that men who cheat usually want to experiment sexually."

"Then you know nothing. They want the intimacy that they don't have with their wives."

Alison took a deep breath, climbed back onto her bed and drew her knees up to lie in a foetal position. She was fed up of her life; she didn't want these feelings any longer.

"We will speak later, Alison," Dr. Horne said, as she left Alison to her thoughts.

In the isolation of her room, Alison felt as

though she was standing at the edge of a deep pool that she was about to plunge into, unable to swim. She jumped out of bed searching for a knife or anything sharp to cut herself, so that she could bleed to death. She needed to end the trap that her brain had caused her to be in. But there were no sharp implements to be found; the room was practically sterile.

Moving her hands to her ears, she realised that her earrings had been removed. Somebody had stolen them. She couldn't even use those to harm herself.

She climbed back onto her bed and placed her hands over her ears, trying to block out the memories of her mother's drunken rages, when she would force pills into Alison's mouth and make her swallow them. Her parents' deaths had released her, but to what? She would forever be taunted by what they had done to her. Her father had been no different, too drunk to defend her from her mother's abuse. When he was sober, he was firm but fun, but the reality was that he was rarely sober. They had told her that she was lucky to be their daughter, and she'd been foolish enough to believe them when they told her that she was to blame with her stupid illness, and that she should be grateful to have such loving parents who tried to help her and put up with her crazy ways. They'd been the most important people in her life, but she now knew that they had been so wrong in how they'd treated her. She had no idea how to help herself. And so to die was now the only answer.

She slapped herself hard around the face, just like her mother would have done. She wanted to ransack the room but there was nothing to destroy. It was all too clinical and safe, so instead she slapped herself even harder.

"I'm sorry, Mummy," she cried.

How could she not know right from wrong? She wanted to fight but there was only herself to fight with. The door was locked. She couldn't escape.

She screamed, "I'm sorry, Mummy. Please let me out."

Banging the door and kicking it with frustration had no effect. It just would not open.

A few minutes passed, and then she sat down on the floor and broke into hysterical laughter. It didn't take long for Dr. Horne to return to Alison's room. She helped Alison to her feet and walked her back towards her bed.

"Don't worry, Alison. We can help you feel better … with time."

"Are you a virgin, Dr. Horne?'

"No, Alison. I'm married with two children."

"Do you know what real love is?" Alison asked with a pained look on her face.

Dr. Horne ran her fingers over Alison's medical notes, which she was holding in her other hand.

"Yes, my dear, and I'm sure that one day you will as well."

"What does it say about me in your notes?"

Taking a deep breath, Dr. Horne replied, "You are very ill, Alison, but you are in the right place. We can help you."

"My life hasn't been great. I wish I could die."

"You don't have to be afraid any longer. We will help you."

"The crazy part is, I'm crazy enough to miss my parents."

"At home, what do you do in your free time, Alison?"

"Antony! I think I love Antony."

"Why do you think that is?"

"Because he accepts that I'm different."

"Tell me about some of your memories."

"I don't have any brothers or sisters. I was a mistake."

"Did you have any pets as a child?"

"I'm scared of cats and dogs."

"Why do you think you struggle so much with life?"

"Because I'm awkward. I just don't fit in."

"Is there anything you'd like to do with your life if you were given the chance?"

"A flower restaurant! I want to open my own restaurant ... full of flowers. I love flowers."

"What a lovely idea. Where would that restaurant be?"

"I don't know. I haven't been to many places, but somewhere in the UK or Europe."

"Maybe a big city would be a good place to open a restaurant?"

"I don't know. I was thinking more like a small village."

"Spot on! I think a village setting would be lovely for a flower restaurant."

"It would be full of charm and character."

"Wow! It sounds amazing."

"It would be unique."

"It sounds really lovely, Alison."

"People will come from everywhere for lunch and dinner."

"It sounds like you have a plan … something to look forward to … something to live for."

"I don't know if I have the time … or the energy."

"It's up to you, Alison, to make your dream come true."

"I don't know if it makes sense."

"One step at a time. Then it won't seem like such a daunting idea. Getting well is the first step."

"Yes, I would love to feel well."

"This is a safe base for you to start to feel better."

"Will it be hard?"

"Just take it easy, and you'll be fine."

"Thank you. I want your help."

"We will make a workable plan."

"Do you really think it could work … that I could feel well?"

"Do you like reading? I could get you some books."

"Do you have any recipe books? I could start thinking about what I would like to put on the menu at my restaurant."

"Yes, I can find some of those, but I think it would be good for you to focus on some other reading as well."

"Yes. It was foolish of me just to say recipe books."

"Your brain just needs some fresh ideas … new ways of looking at things."

"Can you fix my brain?"

"I believe so. But we need to start with some simple strategies."

"Life's been a long struggle."

"Well then, let's make it more pleasurable for you … in a good way."

"Can I get out of this hospital attire and have my clothes back?"

"Not in this part of the hospital. But when you improve and move on to the main ward, you will be able to wear your own clothes again."

"Can I get some food, please? I didn't eat my breakfast."

"Sure! I'll get the nurse to bring you some. I'll come back and see you later, and I'll make sure you get some books. I do have to inform you that you have been sectioned to stay in this unit for a minimum of sixty days for assessment and review, but we can discuss all of that when you are starting to feel a little better. There is no need to worry about that at the moment. Let's just focus on getting you well."

"What happened? How did I get here? I can't remember."

"I'm afraid you lost your husband, Bryan, in an accident and the trauma has made you very ill."

Alison became outraged.

"I didn't! You fucking liar! I don't want to fucking well see you again. Get out! Get out of my room!"

She watched as Dr. Horne left her room and locked the door behind her.

'Good job,' Alison thought. *'I wanted to hit her.'*

A few minutes later, she calmed down and started to feel uneasy about what Dr. Horne had said. She sat on her bed and started to rake at her skin with her fingernails. She itched like mad all over. *'This bed must be full of bedbugs,'* she thought. It was hardly a thrilling thought to be locked in this godforsaken room. They were treating her as if she was some type of delinquent. If only she could find something to kill herself with, it would all be over. She wished her parents hadn't made the mistake of creating her.

Suddenly overcome with tiredness, she lay down and closed her eyes. She hated being on her own. It reminded her of all the times she had been locked in the house on her own when she was a child, and also dreading her mother coming home when the violence would start. It was all her fault; she had been a burden to everyone all of her life. Nobody believed her. It was pointless trying to explain to anyone.

Was she really such a bad person? Nobody understood her. It was hopeless expecting help from anywhere. Doctors just looked at her as some kind of novelty until they got bored with her and then tossed her on the scrap heap. No wonder she had issues with aggression. What did they all expect of her? They all thought that she was mad, but actually it was everyone else who was maddening. They all got on her nerves. Her body tensed and she started to tremble. Why were they all so infuriating? Why couldn't they understand her and help her? It wasn't that she didn't try to feel better.

She punched herself in the stomach to try and relieve some of the worry. She knew that she was getting worse, but she was unable to stop the downward spiral. 'Angry and difficult' was how they all had described her, but none of them really understood what she'd gone through, particularly as a teenager. She'd been in one of these residential treatment facilities before, when she was sixteen; in fact her sixteenth birthday had been spent there. Reckless destruction had been her charge that time. Was this now her destiny … to remain here for the rest of her life? Why couldn't she just find some peace within herself? If only she could just die. She punched her breasts with her fists as tears rolled down her cheeks. Death was the answer, she knew it. She would never be able to feel well. There was no chance.

She rubbed her earlobes. How dare they steal her earrings.

Sniffing her fingers, she was disgusted by the smell of cheese. Why did her fingers smell of cheese? When had she last showered? She fingered her hair. It was full of grease. She started to scratch herself again.

Closing her eyes, the visions began to appear. Black flashes, then white, followed by red, and then pink. Then the faces started. People she'd never met. A demon appeared, its face and torso taunting her. Its hands moved towards her throat. It froze in space and started to laugh. She opened her eyes, but the demon was still there, hovering over her, evil and vile. Its eyes pierced straight through her. It spoke.

"We'll get you yet, Alison."

Freaked out and scared, Alison began to scream. A nurse in a white uniform entered the room.

"Are you okay, Alison. Do you want me to give you something to help calm you?"

"Get it to go away, please."

"I can give you some medication to help."

Alison closed her eyes. "Yes, please … anything. Just make it go away."

The medication began to work. The demon left her room, and with her eyes closed, the images were more pleasant … bright lights around a beautiful flower garden. She drifted off into an overtired sleep, and her body relaxed.

The following day, Alison found herself in Dr. Horne's office, where for the past hour, she had cried, ranted and generally released a lot of her emotions. Dr. Horne had sat patiently and listened.

"I fail at everything," Alison said.

"I think you just have more difficulty than most people at working things out in your own mind. We are here to offer you the support that you need now."

"You mean that you still believe there's a light at the end of the tunnel for me?"

"Yes. With some effort from yourself, you will be able to feel a lot better."

"So, where do we start?"

"By talking … turning negative thinking to a more positive way of thinking."

"So, I shouldn't give up hope? I shouldn't wish to die?" Alison pondered.

"We need to go back over your childhood … pick things apart and then put them back together … for you to have some understanding."

"So, I have to talk about myself as a child?'

"Yes, so that you can make sense of the world around you."

"A lot of things happened in my childhood."

"It won't be a simple undertaking, Alison. It will be difficult and will take huge commitment from you."

"I'm not expecting a fairy-tale. Nobody's managed to help me yet."

"We need to find out how much of your problem stems from your upbringing to establish a true diagnosis."

"And then my head will start to feel better?'

"It's possible that you will feel a lot better."

"It'll be hard for me to talk about a lot of the stuff."

"Yes, trauma is difficult to talk about, and you may have blocked a lot of it out."

"Other people have usually let me down or hurt me."

"We need to find a way to help you not to have such dark thoughts."

"I don't want to stay here forever. My future terrifies me. That's why I wish I could die."

"Your future is capable of being much better than your past."

"I think I'm very scarred, mentally."

"I'm not going to lie to you, Alison. This isn't going to be easy."

"I'm just happy that you're offering me some help."

"The first thing that you need to do is learn to love yourself."

"What's happened to all my stuff that I left at the guest house … and my phone? I need my phone."

"Your belongings are in storage. Once you

are more balanced, you will be able to have them back."

"Antony will want me to be in touch. He'll be wondering what's happened to me."

"Social interactions outside of here would not be good for you at the moment, Alison. I think that, by the sounds of it, your mother always made you feel like an outsider in every social situation."

"Yeah, I was a pain … mentally unstable. I was never good enough."

"She gave you a label … one which has stuck with you."

"I could never do anything right."

"Yes, she has done you a lot of damage."

"Ungainly and awkward was how she would introduce me to the people we met."

"Do you understand, Alison, that she did this to make herself feel superior?"

"She said I was an attention seeker."

"We need to find a way of silencing your mother's voice in your head. Her words weren't true."

"But there *is* something wrong with me. I'm totally dysfunctional."

"You're aggrieved, Alison. We can try and

sort this out."

Alison gave Dr. Horne a fake smile. "I see spirits a lot."

"I believe that's a consequence of your depression and the uncontrollable rage within you."

"There are times I'd like to get hold of a gun and shoot myself in the head to make it all stop."

"The therapy we are going to offer you will help you to stop feeling that way."

"I fail at everything, so I know I'll fail at therapy."

"There's another way of thinking, Alison. A more positive way."

"I don't want to take medication. It doesn't help. Sometimes it even makes me worse."

"The medication I've prescribed will help with the suicidal thoughts."

"Do you really believe you can save me?"

"As I said earlier, yes, but it won't be easy."

"But I'm so messed up ... crazy."

"Wrong, Alison. Admittedly, you need help, but I don't believe that you are crazy."

"I'm nothing but trouble."

"You've hit rock bottom, so the only way is up from here."

Without warning, Alison burst into tears.

"I know it hurts, Alison, but you have to face the truth."

A heavy, leaden feeling lay in Alison's chest. If only she could change. If only she could awaken from this horror, this sadness, this fear. Why did she feel so haunted?

Why wouldn't it all just go away?

Confused, awkward and weird … why was she all of these things? Why did she feel so uncomfortable? Her tears became uncontrollable.

Dr. Horne broke her thoughts.

"This afternoon, I would like you to rest in your room. Read one of the books I left you if you feel up to it, but the most important thing I would like you to do is to write a letter to your mother. Obviously, she's never going to read it, but I would like you to share it with me so that I can gain some insight into your thoughts."

Back in the solitude of her room, Alison took pen to paper.

Dear Mum,

You have left me with so many inner demons. I don't want to write this letter, but Dr. Horne insists it will help me. Not that you're going to read it anyway. Why did you hit me so much? You robbed me of my childhood, my life. Have you any idea what it feels like? I can't describe how unhappy I am. I don't even want to get out of bed anymore. The demons drive me now. I wish I wouldn't wake up tomorrow. Why couldn't you have been different? Why didn't you love me? Living with you was like living in a war zone. I never knew when you were going to attack me next. I wish I could stop my head from thinking. Do you remember the time you tied me up in chains and left me tied to a chair in the cellar, in the pitch dark for over a day and a night? The demons scared me then, like they still do now. You would go to work and leave me, a little girl, all alone, locked up in an empty house. Why? I can't kill the demons. They are inside of me. Do you remember? Of course, you don't! You've left this world. Left me in this mess, all alone. I have no defence, nothing to shield myself with. But then I never did around you. The demons will get me. They keep promising me that.

Your lost daughter, Alison.

Alison lay on her bed; she had never felt so alone. The fear she felt was overwhelming, but writing the letter to her mum had felt good. Her room was cool, so she pulled the blanket up higher to cover herself up. She could hear the wind blowing outside of her window, the one with the iron bars that made it feel like a prison cell. At least in here, she was safe; nobody could hurt her apart from the demons. She felt like a child again, locked in, entirely out of her depth. She comforted herself with the thought that at least the outside world could not get in here to harm her. It was an embarrassment to find herself locked in here.

The spirit of a young woman came to her. She'd been killed in a scooter accident. She was in her early 30s – pretty, with dark hair.

She was laughing as she said, "Life is just too short."

She showed Alison the accident, how the lorry had hit her scooter. She'd died instantly.

The young woman hung up some party lights and unfurled a picnic blanket.

"Let's celebrate," she said, as she patted the red blanket beckoning Alison to sit beside her.

She opened a jewellery box and removed a necklace, which she offered to Alison. Starting to sweat, Alison threw her own blanket off her bed.

"Enough is enough! Leave me alone," Alison shouted.

The woman's doll-like face peered back at her

as she offered Alison a bunch of flowers.

"Stop!" Alison screamed.

Suddenly, Alison was underneath the waves of the sea. Was she dreaming? Something was weighing her down. She was unable to surface.

Horrible droning noises started in her ears. Dead people were floating around her. Tectonic plates were shifting beneath her. A feeling of dread overcame her. Concern filled her, as different colours of light flashed every few seconds. The sea was churning … stormy. Demonic images began to appear, lunging at her and growling. A beam of light emitted from above, straight through her body. She was sinking lower and lower.

A nurse sat on Alison's bed comforting her. Unable to speak, Alison just stared at her.

"Are you okay, Alison?"

"I don't know why I'm crying."

Pausing, the nurse smiled at her. "It's okay, to cry. We all cry sometimes."

"What should I do?"

The nurse glanced at the security camera situated in the corner of Alison's room. "I could give you something to help you sleep."

Alison's eyes rolled back slightly. "I don't

want to end up like a zombie."

"You won't. It will just help you feel more peaceful."

"Do you think I'm mad?'

"If you keep asking that question, then people will think you are. By the way, my name's Leta. I forgot to introduce myself properly when I came in."

"I'm hungry. How long until dinner? And how long do I have to stay in this side room, away from everybody else in here?'

"It's routine for you to be in here … until you learn to relax."

"Routine for whom? Are there others like me?"

"It's called transition … just until we feel you are safe."

Inner turmoil caused Alison's head to spin, but outwardly she smiled at the friendly nurse.

"You're very young to be a nurse working somewhere like this."

"I'm older than I look. I'm probably about the same age as you, I would think." She smiled back at Alison.

"Dinner isn't for another couple of hours, but I could get you a cup of tea and some toast, if you like?'

Still smiling, Alison said, "Thank you, that would be great. I'm starving."

Leta left the room. The lock turned. The smile left Alison's face and was replaced by a feeling of anger at the thought of how long she may have to spend locked in this room. Leta had said it would be until they felt she was safe. That could be for ever.

Her spine tingled as she thumped her fists into her mattress. She had to put on an act … smile all of the time … be pleasant to the nurses. This was her only way out of here. Dr. Horne had said that they would help her. Well, she'd let them do just that … make her feel better.

Itching, Alison started to scratch until she had made the skin on her left leg crack and become painful. She quickly hid it under the bed sheet.

Trumpets sounded all around her. The noises were starting to get to her again.

Chapter 10

Alison started to get to know the personalities of the nurses who looked after her. Leta was her favourite. Some of them she thought of as tough and some as soft. Leta was the softest of them all. One of the tough ones was in fact quite a bully towards Alison. Her name was Mina. Alison knew that she told lies, and enjoyed humiliating her by calling her demeaning names, just like her mother had done. Alison decided to grin and bear it for the time being, but her time would come.

Her days were mixed. On some, she felt much better, but on others, she could end up right back where she'd been when she'd first arrived. She called her bad days her 'nonsense days'.

Most days, she still had interaction with Dr. Horne, but now a second doctor, Dr. Eliott, was also assessing and working with her. Most of the work had involved trying to look inside herself and work out her emotions and trigger points. There was still no talk of when, or even if, she would ever be able to leave the hospital. Once a week, she also sat in what they called a mentor group with other patients.

Today Alison had woken up feeling particularly down. Her bad mood was one she was finding difficult to snap out of. The dark clouds were all around her. Guilt was the driving force behind the way she felt. The intense counselling she had received over the last month had brought back memories of her vicious attack on Darren's wife, and she was full of regret for her actions towards her. Brooding, she stood repeatedly kicking her bed frame. Why was she such a failure? She felt even more disconnected from reality, every day she spent in this place. She hoped that Mina wasn't on duty today, as she didn't think she'd be able to handle her annoyances. But part of her wished that she would be, and that she could beat the hell out of her for how she'd treated her.

She had no contact with the outside world, and was still wrapped in a bubble in her small room, still considered unsafe for the main ward, despite having conducted herself reasonably well at the mentoring group.

Her door opened and Dr. Eliott entered.

"Morning, Alison. Shall we go for a walk outside today? It's a beautiful day."

As they walked together in the delightfully planted garden, Alison's mood shifted. These were her favourite moments, when she was allowed to walk amongst the flowers. She hopped along the stepping stone garden path, breathing in the different scents.

Turning to Dr. Eliott, she said, "Flowers are magical aren't they?"

"Why don't you tell me about how you are feeling today, Alison?"

"Can't we talk about you today? I don't want to spoil my time out here," Alison bent down to smell the flowers.

Dr. Eliott cleared her throat, "Me, you want to talk about me. Okay, that's fine. We'll reverse the roles, out here, whilst we are in the garden. You get to ask me the questions."

"I want to know what makes you and me different?" Alison asked.

"In which case why don't I tell you things about me and in return you try and describe what you feel is different or if actually we are more similar than you believe."

"Okay. You start then," said Alison.

"I'm hard-working, which makes me successful at my job."

"I worked hard at the restaurant as a waitress, but I hated it. I guess you got qualifications to do what you do and I didn't. So if I want to open my flower restaurant, I need to educate myself more about business and things."

"My friends say that I am witty and I have a good sense of humour."

"I don't have any friends, so I need to work out why I can't make friends easily. I'm not sure about humour, I don't think I always get it."

"I'm confident because I understand myself."

"Well, I've clearly got a lot to learn there, 'cos I don't understand myself at all."

"I'm passionate, and I care about people."

"So am I about flowers and art and music, oh and food. I'm not sure, I know how to care about people though."

"I'm modest and humble."

"Well, I don't even know what that means."

"I'm honest."

"I can be, but I can be deceitful if I need to be."

"I'm loving, I care for my friend's, and family

and even people I've never met."

"I don't understand love, I think 'cos I've never been shown."

"I'm responsible."

"I don't think I am."

"I'm reliable."

"I'm getting bored now, can we just finish the walk in silence, please."

They reached the rose garden, a favourite part of the gardens for Alison. The roses were laid out informally and she liked that they were planted randomly, with no structure, giving it a feel of being wilder and less contrived. Flowering shrubs were interspersed with small woodland trees.

Back in Dr. Eliott's office, Alison's therapy started like any of her daily sessions, but today was different as they were going to use hypnotherapy. Alison found herself in a state of trance; it felt pleasant, calm and relaxing.

A rollercoaster of emotions and memories whirled through her mind, and she was unaware that she was speaking.

Dr. Eliott remained quiet, as she made notes in her notepad and Alison dug into the darkest recesses of her subconscious, unlocking some of her terrible memories.

Awake and alert now, Alison found herself studying the details on her own hands. She rubbed the forefinger of her right hand over the scar on her left hand, in the space between her thumb and forefinger.

Alison looked up from her hands, "My whole life has had a darkness around it. I'm just so lost."

"By sharing these feelings, we will be able to help you."

"But you can't protect me, can you?"

"You are safe here."

"I don't feel safe, I'm terrified. Sometimes I used to barricade myself in the bathroom to avoid my mother's violent outbursts."

"That must have felt very lonely for you to have to do that. What age were you when you started to do that?"

"I'm not sure, maybe six or nine. I don't know."

"How are you finding the mentorship group, do you think it's helping you in anyway?"

"I find it comforting that others have gone through bad childhood experiences."

"I've noticed that during the sessions so far, that you have been reluctant to speak."

"That's 'cos I feel so angry when I hear what's happened to the others and I don't know what to do with that anger."

"Well, that's not a bad thing because it shows that you care about the bad things that have happened to them, and not just about yourself."

"It breaks my heart to hear some of it."

"You could always cry to let some of that anger emotion release, when you feel it.'

"Do you think that our destiny's are already written before we are born?" Alison asked.

"I have a vague unease around that that idea, as I believe our outlook and attitudes towards life can change our destiny."

Alison felt herself becoming irritated by Dr. Eliott, "Can we end the session, I've had enough for today."

Locked back in her room, Alison had no way of escaping her thoughts, and the demons were closing in, again. Her door opened, and Mina entered her room with her lunch. Mina's facial expression looked as though she had stood in something unpleasant. She placed the tray of food on the bedside table, "Got those demons in our head again today have we?"

"Fuck off, bitch," Alison retorted.

"You disgust me, every time I look at you, it makes me want to throw up," Mina said.

Alison clenched her fists, "Watch your back, 'cos one of these days I'm going to get you."

"Yeah, and where will that get you? You can't even get to main ward, as it is. Touch me and you'll be locked in here forever."

Mina picked up Alison's water jug and poured water all over her lunch, "Oh dear! Sorry, I spilled some water on your lunch."

Shaking with rage, Alison screamed, "Get out! Get out of my room!"

As Mina left the room, Alison hurled the tray towards the closing door. She needed to formulate a plan; she'd get that bitch one of these days.

Agitated, Alison paced around her room, the ghosts of her feelings thumping inside her head. A monstrous rage was growing deep within her mind. All fear was now abandoned. The memories and nightmares of her childhood came flooding in. The devil was at play with her thoughts, her fragility, as she pondered what type of accident, Mina could die from. How dare she make her feel even more inadequate than she already did, and put her under such enormous pressure to do her some harm. Her mind began to examine all types of scenarios, where Mina may cease to live. She murmured, "Help me Satan, to get her."

With sheer frustration at not being able to harm Mina at that very moment, Alison gave herself one thunderclap of a slap to her own face.

She began to wail, a high-pitched howl. She hated that stupid fat nurse, with that macho, short, spiky haircut. If she didn't get out of this room soon, she was going to end up crazier than she already was. She walked to the window with the iron bars and stared at freedom. Feeling calmer after a few minutes, she began to understand just how much damage, her own mother had inflicted upon her, and she knew that this was a very important message to hold on to. She was broken, but she could heal. She climbed into her bed, pulled up the sheets, and fell asleep listening to the birds, outside of her window.

The following day, Dr. Horne was leading the group session and although Alison was determined to contribute, she had a twisting feeling in the pit of her stomach. So far, she'd remained quiet and let the other three patients make their contributions. They sat on plastic chairs, in a circle, beams of sunlight shone from the ceiling high windows, making the one woman Joyce, look as though she had her own personal stage spotlight shining on her, as she spoke, "I don't think people tend to be all evil or all good, I think some of us just tend to lean more towards evil, when we've had bad things happen to us in our lives."

Dr. Horne pushed her for more, "So you don't think anyone is born to do cruel and horrible acts, but it is how they are treated in life that makes them do these things, Joyce?"

"Yes, I think if you've been shown violence, you're more likely to become violent."

"Do you feel anger drives this?" Dr. Horne asked.

"Yes, it stems from a disturbed mind," Joyce continued.

"Do you believe that it makes you misread certain situations, and overreact?"

"Yes, you lose all sense of reason, and that's if you even had any in the first place."

"Do you think that makes you as bad as the perpetrators who did the bad things to you in the first place?"

"No, because the ones who do that to children are monsters. I'm not a monster, I'd never hurt a child."

"So should we feel sorry for you, even though

you've committed a violent crime against another human being?"

"No, but you should listen and at least understand why."

"Do you feel like a victim yourself, Joyce?"

"Indeed."

Taking Alison by surprise Dr. Horne asked Alison if she would care to make any comment.

Ten seconds went by, "Well, we're all just a bunch of losers," Alison said.

Joyce retorted, "Why are you so full of hate towards everyone here?"

"Hate's too strong a word, if I hated you, I'd kill you," Alison said.

"I think Alison's just having a bad day. Are you feeling a bit irritable, Alison?" Dr.Horne asked.

"I just don't see the benefit to listening to everyone else's problems, when I've got enough of my own to deal with," Alison said.

"Let's all just take a moment here, and try and help Alison understand what her issue is, here." Dr. Horne said.

"I think she needs to take some deep breaths and learn to smile more," Joyce said.

Alison cringed, even here amongst women

like herself, she was different, she didn't fit in. She felt sick to her stomach. She stood up.

Feeling trapped, she looked around her, confused. Her eyes settled on Joyce, a feeling of deep dislike for the woman, overcame her. What gave her the right, to feel like a victim?

A raging heat coursed through her, as her heart thumped too quickly, causing the blood to rush to her head.

She clenched her fists, and paced the room, back and forth.

Blinking, she looked around her, again, "What am I doing here?" she asked to nobody in particular.

Dr. Horne and the other three patients looked at her puzzled.

"Where am I? Why am I here?" Alison asked.

Dr. Horne stood up, moved towards her and looked her in the eye, "You've become disorientated, that's all."

"Am I crazy?" Alison asked.

Choosing not to answer Alison's question, Dr. Horne gently linked arms with her and guided her back to the safety of her own room

Leta helped her into bed and gave her a mild sedative, which made Alison feel even more confused. Her thoughts drifted to leaves on trees, sunsets, flowers, and Antony. Suicidal thoughts took over, but she had no energy to follow through with any of them. Leta had put a dinner tray at the side of her bed, but she had no appetite. Why did everyone hate her? She stared at the chair, at the side of her bed, just its' presence in her room, annoyed her.

Isolation hit her as Leta left the room, and turned the key in the lock. She missed her parents, but how could that be after all they had done to her?

She began to scream, a blood-curdling peal, loud and high-pitched. The noise alarmed her, so she screamed again.

The demons were back, surrounding her. The one that looked like a serpent was crawling towards her. She would be no match, if he decided to attack her.

Chapter 11

Three weeks passed, and Alison was finally moved to the main ward. She was shown to a twin room, which she was to share with a roommate. Thrilled at the prospect of no longer being locked in a room, she smiled to herself as she kept opening and shutting the door to prove to herself that there was no lock.

She hadn't met her roommate yet, but she was determined that, whoever it was going to be, she would like her, and that they would become friends. She would be nice to her. There was no way she was going to go back to that locked room again.

She definitely needed to earn some brownie points now. She had to prove that they could trust her to be around other patients. She wasn't going to mess this up. Her mental health had improved over the last couple of weeks, and she felt a whole lot better than she had for a long time. The room was much nicer than the one she'd left, and somebody had even put a vase of flowers on the shelf nearest her bed, which made her feel even more cheery than she already did. She was beginning to actually like herself; love was still a long way off, but it was a good start. Dr. Horne and Dr. Eliott had agreed.

A woman's head popped around the door.

"Hello, you must be Alison. I'm your roommate, Carina. If you've got any questions or need any help, I've been here for quite a while, so I know my way around most things here."

They sat opposite each other on their beds, chatting and getting to know one another.

"Did your parents make you feel as though you were a disappointment to them?" Alison asked.

"Yes, everything that went wrong was always my fault."

Alison laughed. "So, they were charmers, just like mine were."

"I hope that we can become friends," Carina said.

"I feel like a little girl again … having my own room … but with someone to share it with this time," Alison said.

"We are both very vulnerable, and we need to respect that of one another," Carina said.

"Yes, I sometimes fall into a dark place. I make errors. I've got lots of flaws," Alison replied.

"As long as we are open and honest with one another, we should be okay," Carina stated.

"I get scared sometimes," Alison said.

"I won't judge you," Carina told her.

"Sometimes, I just want to run away from everybody," Alison said.

"It happens to me as well," Carina said.

"I'm so happy to make a friend. I feel like I can already share my secrets with you," Alison said.

Leta knocked and entered.

"It looks like you two are getting on well."

She gave Alison a sincere smile.

Giving her a thumbs-up sign, Alison smiled back.

"Yeah, we're already becoming friends."

"Well, if there's anything you need, just come and find me."

"Thank you, Leta. Isn't it wonderful that I can come and find you now … that I'm no longer locked in my room!"

Leta left them to continue chatting.

"Tell me more about you," Carina said.

Alison sat upright on her bed and leant slightly forward towards Carina.

"I'm in a mess. I don't even know whether I'm going to be allowed to stay here."

Carina massaged the front of her neck.

"Oh no! What did you do?"

"It's all too much. I attacked a woman and injured her quite badly, and she nearly died."

"Trust me! If you ended up in here instead of a cell, they must have thought you did it because of mental health issues."

"I'm really nervous about it all. I'm terrified I'll have to go to prison."

Alison stretched out on her bed and looked around her new room. It was far more spacious than the room she'd previously been locked in, and far more comfortable and less clinical. It had a TV, a desk, a chest of drawers and a wardrobe.

"When will they give me my own clothes and other stuff back?"

"I got mine back two days after they moved me on to the main ward, but you won't get your phone. They don't like you to have unsupervised contact with anyone outside of here. It's like a prison, but not a prison, if you get what I mean."

"Are we allowed to smoke? I've missed not being able to."

"No. And you can't go outside without supervision either. The lounge facility is available from 9am until 6pm, but at all other times you are expected to be in your own room."

"I've got a case meeting with Dr. Horne and Dr. Eliott tomorrow," Alison said.

"They will do all they can to protect you. They did me. I have to stay here for a minimum of three years and will only be released if they think I'm well enough to fit back into society and not be a danger to anyone else or myself."

"Are you allowed visitors?"

"Yes, my sister comes to visit, and also my best friend, but they are supervised visits. I don't see my parents 'cos I don't want to, and they think it would be bad for me, anyway."

"So we don't get any privacy?"

"No, apart from when we shower or use the

loo."

"Are we considered insane?"

"Yes."

"Does anyone ever commit suicide in here?"

"Yes. People often attempt it. I've tried once, but it doesn't help, 'cos they just stick more time on you."

"You could do it though, couldn't you? It would be easy in here."

"Have you met your lawyer yet?"

"No, not yet. We've both fucked up, haven't we?"

"Yeah, it's a scary thought to think we've ended up here," Carina said.

"It's like a massive nightmare … one that there's no escape from," Alison declared.

"I just hope you get a good lawyer. Mine was fantastic."

"Well, I am guilty of what they've accused me of, but I guess it's going to be down to whether the doctors decide if I'm insane or not. I'm not sure which is best – to be told you're insane or to face prison – but I know one thing's for sure, I'd rather do my time here than in a prison cell with real criminals."

A bell rang.

"C'mon, Alison. That's the bell for dinner. It's pizza tonight."

"But it's only five-thirty."

"Yes, that's when we have dinner. Don't forget we have to be back in our room, by six."

After dinner, Alison found herself on the floor in their room beside Carina, doing pushups and crunches.

"It's vital to exercise to keep yourself fit in here," Carina instructed. "By the way, I like to read for an hour or so after my exercise, so I suggest you find a good book, as I don't like to be disturbed whilst I'm reading."

"I'm thinking I might start writing, especially as we have a desk," Alison said.

"What will you write?"

"Well, I thought I'd start with a love letter to Antony."

"You've got a man?"

"Yes, we've been trying to have a baby together," Alison lied.

Carina rubbed her eyes.

"Oh, my God! You're not pregnant, are you?"

Alison let the thought run in her mind for a moment. A future with Antony and a baby! It was like watching a movie, only she was the star of the show.

"Well, I haven't had a period since I've been here, and I've been here two months now."

Gasping, Carina said, "Holy shit!"

"What happens to babies in maximum security hospitals?" Alison asked.

"I don't know. More freedom for you, I guess ... to be with your baby."

The following morning, Alison was attending the meeting with the two doctors to discuss their assessment of her for the court. Dr. Horne opened the conversation.

"I believe there is more than one persona that resides within your body, Alison."

An eager smile jumped across the desk from Alison to Dr. Horne as she studied the delicate features of the doctor's face.

"There is a dark side to your personality," Dr. Horne continued. "There are many different complex parts. I don't doubt the voices you hear inside your head. Most of this stems from the violent childhood you experienced. Your mother told you from a very young age that you were weird, and this has contributed to your mental state. I believe that you invented characters inside your mind as a means of escape from the reality of the situation you were in."

Dr. Horne gave Alison a warm smile.

Alison was feeling ambivalent about the doctor's words. All she really wanted to know was whether she would be facing trial and prison, or whether she could serve her time in the protective bubble of the hospital.

Dr. Horne spoke again.

"You have very little understanding of personal boundaries, and you suffered a very miserable childhood. Sadly, professionals, who were there to help you, failed you by not recognising the harmful effects on your developing mind. They allowed you to continue to suffer in pain.

"Dr. Eliott, would you like to make Alison aware of your assessment."

"Yes. Thank you, Dr. Horne. Alison, my findings are that I believe a lot of your thoughts and actions are on what I describe as autopilot. You have undoubtedly suffered a lot of mental anguish throughout your life. The relationship with your parents, particularly with your mother, has had a huge effect upon you, which has resulted in your mind finding its own way to distract you from the pain. This has developed into what I consider to be a compulsive personality, where you have little control over your emotions and actions. I believe a deep-rooted anger resides within you."

Staring at the wall, unwilling to make eye contact with Dr. Eliott, Alison blinked repeatedly in an attempt to hold back her tears.

"I am aware that these words must be very uncomfortable for you to hear," Dr. Eliott continued. "The emotions you feel are powerful. But they are often suppressed and in turn result in an overreaction.

"Do you want to ask me anything at this point, Alison?"

"My life rests on your decisions."

Dr. Eliott thought for a moment before she replied.

"Yes, Alison, it does. But we have to rely upon our clinical knowledge and expertise in these matters."

"My whole life is at stake here," Alison said.

"The mind is very complex, Alison. Our job is to peel back the layers, like peeling an onion, to see what lies beneath, in the very depths of your mind."

Alison burst into tears.

"I'm sorry to upset you, but you really have not acknowledged, or come to terms with, your husband's accident. My conclusion is that you are indeed insane at this time. Dr. Horne agrees with me."

The images came in waves, crashing through Alison's mind. She closed her eyes, trying to block them out. Before her, all she could see was a concrete wall. Her mind was out of control. Her heart sank. Her stomach knotted. Her life would be over if she was sent to prison. She would be trapped in a cell for the rest of her life. When would she wake up from this nightmare called life?

Panic struck her. The voices started. She sat mute and numb with fear. Why couldn't she just die? Antony's face flashed across the concrete wall. Her body began to tremble. Antony's kind eyes winked at her. She opened her own terrified ones.

"I'm scared," she said.

Dr. Horne tried to comfort her.

"Your mental health is our priority whilst you remain here. We realise that the uncertainty of how long you will reside here is likely to unsettle you emotionally, and we will keep a very close eye on you over the next few days. We feel that sharing a room with Carina will be more beneficial to you at the moment, than being isolated in your own room. But, if at any point you would prefer to have your own space, then please speak to one of us, and this can be quickly arranged."

"I think I might be pregnant," Alison blurted out.

Dr. Eliott glanced at Dr. Horne and then her eyes rested back on Alison's distraught face.

"Well, that statement has certainly blown the lid off Pandora's box."

"What makes you think that you may be pregnant, Alison?" Dr. Horne enquired.

"I've missed two periods since I've been here. I think I've also gained a bit of weight, and considering there are days where I don't eat anything at all, I don't know why this is."

"Could this be another reason why you've been having suicidal thoughts?" Dr. Eliott asked.

Bending forward and putting her head between her knees, Alison mumbled, "I don't think so."

"It's a good thing that you've shared this information with us. There's nothing to be ashamed of," Dr. Horne said.

"I can't have a baby in prison though, can I?"

"There are mother and baby units in hospitals like this, as well," Dr. Eliott explained.

"But that's not okay, is it? To bring a baby up somewhere like that?" Alison asked.

"Decisions would need to be made, certainly, but let's get you a pregnancy test first to establish if you are actually pregnant," Dr. Horne said, glancing over worriedly at Dr. Eliott.

The raging anger was starting to surface at the thought of them trying to take her baby away from her. Yet again, her life had become chaotic.

By 3pm, she was peeing on a white stick to determine whether she was pregnant or not, with Dr. Horne and Dr. Eliott standing outside the cubicle to review the result with her.

'What if she wasn't pregnant?' she thought as she exited the cubicle and handed the stick to Dr. Horne.

They all waited and then Dr. Horne shook her head.

"You're not pregnant, Alison."

In that moment, Alison felt no joy.

"I don't want to have any more 'nonsense days'," Alison said.

"You do understand that there is no baby don't you, Alison?" Dr. Horne asked.

Alison pondered the question. She knew the facts but she couldn't weave them together to make any meaning. The answer to this question wasn't a simple undertaking. The dark thoughts started to roll in. In her head, she could pretend that Antony was the father, but in reality, she knew that it was Darren. The father of her baby was also the husband of the woman she was accused of attacking. She could pretend it was Antony though, couldn't she? The problem was dizzying. She couldn't answer the question. Did it matter if she lied? She wished that Antony was the father. That would have been a much simpler solution.

Frozen in silence, Alison just stared at Dr. Horne. How could she be honest? The tears fell again.

"I won't let the demons win," she sobbed.

"You're not alone in this, Alison. Let's go back to my office. It'll be more private than standing here in the toilets," Dr. Horne said.

Alison sat in the same chair that she always occupied for her therapy sessions with Dr. Horne. The two of them were alone now, Dr. Eliott having left to see another patient.

"The demons still keep coming. I can't

control them."

"So, embrace them. Let them in and then dismiss them. You need to reclaim your power over them."

"It's too scary."

"You *will* face them. You'll find the courage."

"Do you ever see them?" Alison asked.

"Would it surprise you to learn that I also had a chaotic childhood? Not on the same level as your own, but a chaotic one, nevertheless. I've had days, years ago, when I didn't cope very well with life and all the things it threw at me."

"I'm so scared!"

Alison sneezed; she was starting with a cold.

"What if there were some exceptional circumstances around the baby? Well, you won't believe who the fucking father of this baby is."

"There is no baby, Alison."

"Do you think he needs to know the truth?"

"I've found in life that the more truthful and honest you are around situations, the less complex they become."

"Well, the secret's out now anyway, 'cos you already know."

A moment of silence rested between them. Alison looked at Dr. Horne with tears in her eyes.

"Shall we take a walk in the garden, Alison? That always seems to cheer you up."

Face lighting up, Alison smiled at Dr. Horne.

"Thank you," she whispered.

As they walked side by side along the garden paths, Alison turned to Dr. Horne.

"Am I really going to have a baby? It's hard to believe."

Dr. Horne sighed.

"No, Alison. There is no baby."

Alison smiled. "I want to keep it."

She bent over to smell a flower, which had caught her eye.

"I know you are really worried about everything, but I will ensure you get all the help you need."

"People used to shake their heads in disgust at how my mother sometimes treated me in public, and they would smile and nod at me. But they never did anything to try and stop her."

"I'm so sorry, Alison, for all that you have had to put up with during your life."

"When I'm outside, but mainly in places where there are flowers, it's like my mind is different. I feel pleasure. My senses are ignited. To be able to touch, smell and see the beauty of what life can be," Alison said.

"Love can give you joy as well, but this is something you have to learn. We are going to try and help you to love yourself."

"I just wish some of the horrible memories would go away."

"Yes, but going forward in life, you can make happy memories."

"I make such stupid mistakes. My judgement is so clouded."

"Yes, but you can learn from those mistakes."

"Thank you, Dr. Horne. I really like you."

Lifting her face towards the sun, Alison closed her eyes and let herself feel the heat of the sun's rays on her skin. A smile crossed her lips as she breathed in the aroma of the scented flowers. It was one of the brightest moments she had experienced for a long time.

Back in their room, Alison shared the news of her pregnancy with Carina, omitting the fact that Darren was the father and not Antony. It felt good to be able to share and confide in someone she now considered to be her friend.

She had never felt so close to anyone as she did Carina. She could be herself in Carina's presence, as they were so similar in their ways.

"I'm so thrilled for you, Alison. A baby! How lovely! Now we've both got something pleasant to think about. I'm so excited for you."

Smiling at Carina, Alison said," It's like some sunshine has entered my life."

"Aren't you scared, though, about being able to cope and that you might do it harm, like our parents did to us?"

"I know it's going to be challenging, but Dr. Horne said that I will get the help I need. I'll be in a mother and baby unit.

"Shall we listen to some music for a bit?"

Chapter 12

Heartburn was driving Alison crazy, and the morning nausea wasn't the best of feelings either. Today, she was due to have a scan to try and date the gestation of the baby.

She lay quietly on her bed, staring at the whirling blades of the ceiling fan. Her earphones in her ears, she listened to the music from her iPod, trying to dull out the thoughts of the predicament she had found herself in. She felt so tired, because she'd been having difficulty sleeping for the last week.

The thought of the scan was plunging her into a state of panic. She lay still, feeling frozen to the spot. She and Darren had created this baby. That was the reality she had to face. Antony was not the father. She had to keep reminding herself of that fact, although she was still pretending to Carina that he was.

She closed her eyes and her mind drifted into

a shadowy darkness. If only she could escape, find a way out of here and go on the run. She could feel the rage growing inside her. If only she could stay calm … her thoughts not so brutal.

She was so nervous about having the scan. Her mind was broken. How could she expect to be able to look after a small baby? She touched her tummy. She could feel a slight swell. Tears cascaded down her cheeks.

Leta touched Alison's arm, startling her.

"C'mon, Alison. Let's go and walk in the gardens."

Instead of walking in the gardens, though, Alison's mind transported her to a car with a driver. They sat in the back, Dr. Horne one side of her and Leta the other. They took her for her appointment at the maternity hospital. The weather was awful, thunderclaps booming as they drove through the sleepy countryside. Sheets of rain lashed the windscreen, causing the driver to drive cautiously.

Alison's emotions were becoming increasingly unstable as the journey progressed. She was playing the starring role in her own horror movie. She'd eaten no breakfast and she felt sick. She hugged her knees and closed her eyes, trying to block out the image of the black beast creeping before her. Drumbeats banged in her head. Her supressed anger was growing. Her blood boiled. Five minutes later, she was being helped out of the car and escorted to the maternity ward.

She realised that the driver of the car was, in fact, a policeman. They hadn't cuffed her. She could run. But should she run?

The thought was split-second. She didn't just run, she sprinted along the streets. Her mind was wild, untamed. She ran with the speed and determination of an escaping animal. The policeman was slower, as she sped across the ground. He couldn't catch her, and she ran for hours, through the driving rain.

Finally, she allowed herself to stop and sit underneath a tree, whilst she took in her surroundings. She was on a golf course, but where? The black beast she'd seen earlier in the car was heading towards her. It was stalking her, ready to pounce. Its movements were slow and calculated. It was about 20 meters away from her now. On closer inspection, it looked like a big cat: a black panther. Terrified, Alison shuffled backwards, closer to the tree. It looked hungry, as though she was about to be the meal he'd been longing for. She was too frightened to move.

Her heart rate increased, and the palpitations

started, but then the beast turned around and simply disappeared before her very eyes. Exhausted, she tried to get rid of her thoughts. She'd made the decision to run, but where could she hide?

A deep sadness overcame her. Were her thoughts even lucid? What about the baby? Was there even a baby? Again, her life was just one massive nightmare. She needed sleep, but she couldn't sleep here. She needed to find somewhere dry.

She forced herself to move. They would be searching for her, so she headed away from the golf course in the direction that looked the most remote. After about half an hour of walking, she came across a huge barn. She cautiously peered inside. It was full to the brim with grain, but there were no livestock, nor any other people around. Nearby, there were apple trees. She ventured over and took two of the apples from the tree, one to eat now and one to eat after she'd slept.

The rain was easing, and the summer sun was heating up. She felt thirsty, but that would have to wait. She shed her wet clothes and hung them on the tree to dry. It would be better to sleep naked than to lie in wringing-wet clothes. She stood in the sun for a few moments to dry her skin. Hopefully, no farmer would come and disturb her. She didn't want to have to run again today, especially when she was naked. She lay on the floor of the barn, listening to the silence. It felt scary in the barn, but she had no choice if she wanted sleep. She ate the first of the apples, and with the other hand rubbed her feet; they were sore. Though still unrelaxed, she felt more at ease, although the chill of the barn floor made her shiver. Shadows played tricks in the darkness of the barn. She heard a cat 'miaow' but couldn't determine where the sound was coming from.

She sneezed. The cold she was already suffering from was worsening. She couldn't afford to be ill … not now. Had her decision to run been wise? In this comfortless barn, she wasn't sure she'd made the right decision. She swallowed hard. She needed a drink.

She woke to a full moon forming at the edge of the horizon. She must have slept for hours. She thought she heard a voice, but she couldn't be sure. She crept out of the barn, skirting it until she could see the tree with her clothes hanging on it. She ran over, grabbed them and dressed hastily. She was undecided whether to move in the cover of darkness or to wait until first light. The barn was dry, but it was draughty and dusty. A spasm of nausea overcame her. She decided to move. She had to find water or something to drink.

Heading away from the barn, she ventured onto an unpaved footpath. She came across a small town, but it seemed that everyone was asleep. There was a hotel. She longed for a bed there, but with no money and the fact that her face was more than likely splashed all over the news as a fugitive, this was not an option.

Alison turned quickly. She thought she'd heard somebody behind her, following her, but the street was empty. Her heart pounded. She was desperate for a drink. She felt so lonely. If only she had a way of contacting Antony. He'd be able to help her, but she didn't have his number, and she'd never been to his house. All she knew was that it was somewhere in Bournemouth. She felt like screaming, but that would only draw attention to herself.

She knew it wasn't safe to stay in the town, but she didn't know where else to go. She didn't even know where she was. The name of the town on the street sign, Chilliwack, meant nothing to her.

Her body ached. She felt exhausted and irritated. The anger was once again rising within her. She slumped down on the pavement opposite the hotel, filled with despair and emptiness.

Why had she run? She could have been safely in her bed now, next to Carina's, instead of sitting on a pavement, shivering, and feeling thirsty and hungry.

How could she have even expected to survive out here? She had no idea what to do. She was a failure, even at running away. She felt scared and afraid. She began to cry. A feeling of self-loathing overwhelmed her. Why wouldn't her mind allow her to find peace?

She decided she'd sit here and wait, but what was she waiting for? Annoyed with herself, she slapped her face. She glanced up and down the street. Chilliwack, who even gave a name like that to a town?

A cat came towards her for a closer look. She picked up a stone and launched it in its direction.

"Clear off," she shouted.

She looked over at the hotel. Should she go over and wander in? Maybe they'd at least give her a glass of water.

A car alarm further up the street startled her.

"Shut the fuck up," she shouted.

She didn't know how it happened, but she found herself in the reception area of the hotel. Her voice sounded like her own, but she couldn't be sure as she spoke to the receptionist.

"Can I have a glass of water, please? And can you call the police?"

The receptionist fetched her a glass of water and handed it to her.

"Oh, my! You poor thing! Have you been attacked or raped or something? Let me get you a blanket. You're freezing."

Gulping at the glass of water, Alison heard the receptionist speaking into the phone's handset.

"I've a young lady here. She's in quite a state. She's asked me to call the police. Can you come as quickly as you can, please?"

Well, that was her fate sealed then. She'd definitely be going back to the hospital now. But at least she'd have a warm bed and some food.

Everything appeared to be going in slow motion. It was as if Alison's mind was not quite tuned in. She closed her eyes as the room started to spin. Alison's life felt as though it was just one recurring nightmare.

At the sight of the two policemen arriving at the hotel, Alison started to sweat and freak out. The slow motion now seemed to have turned into fast-forward mode. She was terrified. The older of the two policemen spoke first.

"Let's start with some basics. What's your name and address?"

Rubbing her sore, tired thigh muscles, Alison murmured, "Alison … Alison Ware."

Within seconds, she was handcuffed.

"She's the one we've been looking for … the one who escaped yesterday," the younger policeman said.

They led her to the police car and placed her in the back. She didn't know what to say, so she remained silent.

She finally plucked up the courage to speak.

"Are you taking me back to the hospital?"

"No, we'll need to take you to the station, then we'll let the hospital know we've found you and see what they want us to do with you."

"Will I have to go in a cell? I won't feel safe. It'll make me worse than I already am … and also, I'm vulnerable … I'm pregnant."

Both policemen remained silent for the rest of the journey.

Seething with hatred for Darren and his abhorrent wife, Alison closed her eyes, trying to block out her thoughts.

A PARALLEL PERSONA

As the car pulled into the yard at the rear of the police station, she felt sick-to-her-stomach … sick, in fact, of her entire life. She felt uncertain and confused. A fear that they might not take her back to the hospital and just leave her in a cell gripped her to the core. Why did everybody misunderstand her?

Entering the station by the back door, she felt threatened by the presence of the officers. What were their intentions towards her?

"Please don't lock me in a cell," she cried.

The older officer booked her in with the desk sergeant.

"Alison Ware, fugitive from Spring Hill Hospital. Not sure what you want us to do with her. She's terrified of being put in a cell, but I don't see that we have much choice."

"I feel like crap. Please don't put me in a cell. I can't cope. Just let me sit in an interview room or something. I promise I'll behave," Alison said.

"Okay, she can sit in an interview room for now, whilst I contact the hospital. I'll ask if they can send somebody over to escort her back. That would be the best option," the desk sergeant said.

A policewoman sat opposite Alison in the interview room.

"Bloody waste of my time, this is. Sat babysitting you for half the night. I've paperwork to do, and I'll end up having to do overtime to sort it all out 'cos of you."

Studying the floor, Alison forced herself not to respond. She'd promised she'd behave, and she desperately didn't want to end up in a cell.

"You! I'm talking to you! At least look at me when I speak," the policewoman continued.

Alison stared her in the eye and thought, *'If I went for you, you wouldn't stand a chance.'*

"What's your addiction then? What you into? What got you in this mess?" the policewoman asked.

"And what made you such a bitch?" Alison retorted.

The middle-aged, blonde policewoman said, "What do they even do with you nutters up at Spring Hill? Do you just sit and talk to shrinks all day, making them feel sorry for you, making up lies about how badly the world has treated you and how it's everybody else's fault that you've turned out like a piece of shit?"

Blinking in disbelief at the poisonous words that had just come out of the policewoman's mouth, Alison was shocked by her toxicity towards her.

"Why are you being so nasty to me? What did I actually do to you?" Alison asked, tears welling in her eyes.

"Just trying to do my job! But I'm pissed off that I'm having to look after you. You should be in a cell," the policewoman said.

"Well, you could show me a little more respect," Alison said.

"People like you make me angry. Wasters! That's what you are."

The policewoman continued her rant.

Glaring at her, Alison turned bright red with rage.

"Maybe you're the one who needs to see a shrink. Job getting to you, is it?"

"You've no idea. It's the perfect bloody storm, doing what we do."

"Thought so. You've got serious issues, you have," Alison said.

"The amount of trauma we see, it's no wonder we're all half crazy."

"Yeah, well … you didn't need to have such an attitude with me. You know nothing about my life, or who I really am," Alison said.

"It's just really frustrating being stuck in here with you, when I've so much to do."

"Well, at least your life isn't destroyed like mine is," Alison said.

"What's wrong with you, anyway? Why have they got you locked up at Spring Hill?"

"Mental health issues. I've had them since I was a kid."

Alison fidgeted in her chair as she noticed the policewoman look a bit sheepish and embarrassed. She must have realised she'd handled the whole situation badly.

"I'm sorry I was so rude to you. You didn't deserve that."

"I need the loo," Alison said.

The policewoman nodded and escorted her to the bathroom.

"I'll wait outside the cubicle, but don't get any stupid ideas, will you!"

"I won't. I did hand myself in, you know."

From the cubicle, Alison screamed as she spotted a small amount of blood in her knickers.

"I'm bleeding! I'm losing my baby! Get me a doctor!"

Within less than an hour, the police doctor was trying to reassure Alison that everything should be fine. Visibly upset, Alison insisted on being taken back to Spring Hill as soon as possible.

A range of black dots and zigzags flashed before her eyes, and the whole of the right side of her body had a tingling numbness. She felt dizzy and nauseous. Her brain felt as though it was pulsating. The doctor handed her a cold face cloth and told her to place it on her brow.

"I'll arrange to get you back to Spring Hill as soon as we can," the doctor said.

Just the thought of being back at Spring Hill gave Alison sense of relief.

"Please! The sooner the better. I feel so unwell."

Thirty minutes later, Alison was in an ambulance en route to Spring Hill, the police doctor accompanying her in the back.

On arrival, Dr. Horne was waiting for Alison and immediately took her to the single room she had been placed in before.

"I don't want to be in here. I want to go back to the other room with Carina," Alison said.

"I'm afraid that, because of everything that's taken place, that will not be possible at the moment, Alison. We can discuss it further tomorrow, but presently the most important thing for you to do is to take your medication and get some sleep," Dr. Horne said.

"I want to get in touch with Antony to let him know where I am. Please can I have my phone?"

"Not tonight, Alison."

"I want to see him. I'm desperate to see him. I'm sorry. I'm so glad to be back here. Please don't be angry with me," Alison said.

Exhausted, she fell into a deep sleep.

The following morning, she awoke feeling bewildered, confused and ashamed of her actions. Why had she been so stupid as to try and escape? She checked her pants. No more blood. At least, her baby was still safe.

Black shadows started to dance across the walls. Then, a face appeared … the face of a woman turned upward. She looked deranged with her long, dark hair in tangles. Her body materialised wearing a floating black cloak. She was tall, thin and bony. Alison screamed at her with rage.

"Get out of my room and leave me alone."

The woman didn't leave. She taunted her. Alison's eyes followed her around the walls. The woman opened her mouth and jeered. Her prominent teeth looked threatening. The woman's skin was charred as though she'd been in a fire.

For a long time, the woman stared at Alison and said nothing. Black smoke hung around her body as if hugging her. Her fingers were like tendrils, curling and beckoning Alison in her direction.

Alison screamed again, "Go away! You're scaring me, you disgusting creature."

The black eyes of the woman, penetrated into Alison's mind. Then the woman spoke.

"You are a worthless soul."

Alison began to drip with sweat.

"And also a tortured soul. That's what you are," the woman said.

Edging backwards to the locked doorway, Alison banged on the door and screamed, "Let me out! Let me out!"

Mina, the bullying nurse, unlocked the door.

Chapter 13

Already gripped with absolute horror, the sight of Mina entering her room made Alison feel even worse.

"Can I see Dr. Horne? I feel absolutely dreadful, and I keep seeing things in my room."

"Do you think she lives here … spends all her time just waiting for the likes of you to demand to see her whenever you feel the urge? It's bad enough that *I* have to be here at night. Sleep deprived, that's what *I* am."

"I don't think you understand the enormity of my problems. If you did, you'd be a lot more sympathetic towards me."

"I know your emotions are tricky, but you lot aren't the only one's who've had painful things happen to them. Bad things happen to all of us, but it doesn't mean that everybody ends up in a place like this."

Alison could feel her body tensing up.

"Well, you're in a position of authority here. You should try and be kinder."

"Oh, yeah! Tell me why!"

"Seriously, you need to ask yourself that question."

"I'm not here to be your friend. I don't need your opinions."

Shuddering, Alison realised the room had become increasingly cold. She began to scream.

"What's up? Why are you screaming?"

"Demons and spirits! Do you see them?"

Mina laughed.

"They are just paranoid thoughts, that's all. They're not real."

"But they are real. I think one of them is going to harm me … or maybe even you. There's one right behind you now: a shadow standing by the door, staring at me with its bright yellow eyes."

"You're spooking me out now, Alison. So stop it!"

"Can't you hear the voices telling me to do things?"

Moving to the door, Mina said, "I'm off! You

can deal with this on your own. I've heard enough. You need to get some sleep. You're crazier than most of them in here."

She exited the room and locked the door behind her.

"What do you want from me?" Alison screamed.

The shadow with the yellow eyes spoke.

"Alison! Alison! Alison!

"Mina! Mina! Mina!

"Can I touch your hair, Alison?

"She's on the bed … Why is Alison on the bed?"

Her eyes darted around the room. She could no longer see the entity, just hear its voice.

All of a sudden, the lights flashed and went out resulting in complete darkness.

Then, the voice stopped and there was total silence.

Alison sat on her bed, terrified. Nothing made any sense. She could feel them watching her through the darkness. Were they trying to gain control of her mind?

She felt unnerved and she started to panic as a hollow-eyed skull appeared in front of her. She froze as it hovered before her. The silence was absolute. The air was still. She stared at its fang-like teeth.

Things remained like this for what seemed to be the best part of an hour. Then, she could stand it no longer.

"Help me! Somebody help me!" she screamed.

The skull's mouth opened.

"I'm sorry. I'm sorry," it said.

Continuing to stare at it in horror, Alison felt the room chill even further. She screamed even louder.

The door opened and Mina entered.

"What the fuck! You'll wake the whole bloody hospital."

She switched on the light.

"There was a skull at the bottom of my bed," Alison whispered, her voice becoming fainter as she spoke.

Mina remained speechless.

"I was so scared. Please help me, Mina. I thought I was going to be attacked. It was like I was frozen to the bed."

"I'll get you a cup of tea," Mina said in a softer voice.

A smell caught Alison off guard. Urine! She looked down, horrified. She'd wet herself.

She gingerly climbed off the bed, wondering how she could hide this fact from Mina on her return. She was halfway across the room when Mina came back with the cup of tea.

Mina sniffed the air.

"Oh my goodness! Have you wet yourself?"

Jerking back towards the wall, Alison mumbled, "I'm sorry!"

The pervasively astringent reek of urine hung in the air. She held her hands in tight fists at her sides, embarrassed that she'd been caught before she'd had a chance to hide the evidence.

"C'mon don't look so mortified. Let's freshen you up."

"My whole life's just one long nightmare."

Alison gasped for air.

"Breathe! Take some deep breaths. It will help you to get everything back under control."

"Am I so crazy? Can't you see or hear them, Mina? Am I so flawed ... so dysfunctional? Why are you being so kind to me now?"

"It's my job that stinks, not you. I just hate it so much, I sometimes take it out on you lot. Some of what you said earlier tonight struck a bit of a chord with me. I do need to try and be kinder. It's just that I'm always so busy. There's never enough staff here."

Mina bit the inside of her cheek.

Drawing a deep breath, Alison sighed. She could feel the tears beginning to form. Her mind had taken a journey into Mina's emotional core.

"Hey, hey, hey! Don't you start crying on me now," Mina said.

Chapter 14

The following morning, Alison was escorted down the long corridor to Dr. Horne's office. As they walked, Alison wept. She could see faces staring out at her from every inch of the stark white walls.

Dr. Horne opened the conversation.

"It seems as though you're feeling far worse than you have for a while?"

"I know. It's terrible. I'm so worried about having this baby."

"There is no baby, Alison. We are here to support and guide you. It's important for us to keep you healthy and to make safe choices on your behalf."

Alison wasn't listening.

The one simple question about what might have happened to her baby had, in her mind, turned into 20 questions. The battle within her was turning into a war.

She started to hum, then picked up the glass paperweight from Dr. Horne's desk and ran her fingers over it. Staring at Dr. Horne, she screamed.

"Scream away, Alison. Get rid of all that pent up emotion."

The reaction from Dr. Horne took her by surprise. She stopped screaming.

"I don't have anything nice to say."

"That's okay. Don't ignore that inner voice."

"Well, I know I'm not socially normal."

"I think you are frustrated with yourself, because you were making progress here, and now you have taken a tumble backwards."

"I feel so angry and stressed with myself. I'm living a nightmare of fear, dread and impending doom."

"You're more resilient than you realise."

Breaking down in tears, Alison said, "What if I've harmed my baby."

"There is no baby, Alison."

Overcome with emotion, Alison cried even more.

Dangerous-looking, dark shifting shapes

were dancing all around the walls and creeping across the floor.

One of them looked directly at her and murmured, "I died recently."

The face was blank.

"We have company," Alison said.

Looking uncertain, Dr. Horne responded, "What do you mean?"

Fidgeting in her chair, Alison said, "You'll just say I've lost the plot if I explain."

"It's okay if you have something controversial to say."

Bright red orbs flashed across the walls, accompanied by a high-pitched wailing. The tension was rising within Alison. Two spirits she had never seen in her life before stood either side of Dr. Horne. One was a chubby woman with short spiky hair, the other a man dressed in a shirt and tie.

The woman spirit spoke.

"I have an important message for you: broken things can heal."

She winked at Alison, who closed her eyes trying to shut it all out.

"What is it, Alison? Why have you closed your eyes?" Dr. Horne asked.

A PARALLEL PERSONA

A shiver ran down Alison's spine. The thick atmosphere of the other world was almost choking her, and a swarm of faces with horns danced before her, tormenting her mind.

The sound of a phone ringing disturbed her thoughts. She opened her eyes.

Dr. Horne picked up the receiver.

"Sorry, I need to take this," she said, holding her hand over the mouthpiece.

Alison's face twitched.

"When I was growing up and dreaming of my adult life, this isn't what I had in mind," she mumbled.

Dr. Horne finished her conversation and hung up the phone.

"Your life isn't over, Alison. It's not to say you can't ever be a productive member of society."

"It feels as though I'll always be in some type of conflict with myself. I guess my dream of owning a flower restaurant one day is just pie in the sky."

Looking Alison in the eyes, Dr. Horne said, "Don't give up. Let us help you whilst you are here."

"I suppose I need to attempt to better

understand the world around me, but what if it's all a lie?"

"Just remember that everything you do over the coming weeks will affect where your future lies."

"I don't have control over my thoughts. What should I do? My life is a complete disaster."

"We need to begin by helping you to face yourself ... to face your inner fears."

"I want to see Antony. Can you contact him for me, please?"

"You're in a vulnerable position, Alison. It's not wise to see anyone from the outside world at the moment."

"I can't control what he does, or whether he chooses to see me. But what I do know is, he's an extraordinary man."

"I want you to remain in the privacy of your own room for one week, but also to join in the group sessions. If you can behave for this week, I'll consider moving you back onto the main ward, sharing with Carina again."

"Thank you. I so want to see her. I was so much happier having somebody to talk to, somebody who seemed to understand me."

Over the following week, determined to get

herself back onto the main ward with Carina, Alison developed a routine to help get her through the days. Every day, she awoke telling herself that this was going to be the best day ever. After showering and breakfast, she would read for a couple of hours – mainly her recipe books – and she would dream about the restaurant she would one day own. Just before lunch, she would have a therapy session with either Dr. Horne or Dr. Eliott. She trusted and respected Dr. Horne and her relationship with Dr. Eliott was improving. After lunch, she would write out menus for her restaurant, a different one each day. She would then take a 30-minute afternoon nap, which she discovered helped to improve her mood. After her nap, she would do 30 minutes exercise. Dinner would usually be served around this time, and afterwards she would meditate for 30 minutes. For the rest of her evening, she would listen to music until 'lights out', when she would thank the spirits and voices for having not interfered with her day, and she asked them not to disturb her sleep.

As the week, in which she needed to prove she could behave, came to a close, Alison attended her daily therapy session with Dr. Horne, but in her own mind she was sitting in the visitor's room of the hospital, marvelling at the fact that Antony was sitting opposite her.

On his arrival, he'd hugged her and kissed her on the cheek, before taking the only other chair in the room. She was relieved that they'd allowed her to be on her own with him. It made the situation far less stressful.

He opened the conversation.

"So, they've told me their story, but what's going on here?"

"It's complex. I've got myself in an absolute mess."

"Did you relapse with your schizophrenia?"

"My emotions have been horrendous."

"I'm so sorry. I wish I'd known sooner. They only called me this morning. I've been calling your phone, but it was saying it was switched off. The guesthouse couldn't give me any information; it was like you'd just vanished into thin air. I've been so worried about you."

"Thank you for caring about me so much, and for coming today. You've no idea how much this means to me."

"I'm just so relieved to have found you. I had images of you lying dead in a ditch somewhere." He flashed her a smile. "So now I'm here, what can I do to help?"

"You've helped me already by just turning up to see me."

"I'm worried about you. They said you're here because you attacked a woman."

"It's not that black-or-white. Yes, I did attack her, but she attacked me first."

"What evidence do you have that she attacked you first?"

"I'm uncertain. I guess none, as her husband was the only witness."

"I'm not judging here, by the way. I'm just trying to understand how the hell you've ended up in this place."

"It's all so overwhelming. I don't know where to start."

She straightened her back in the chair.

Chapter 15

"Love is mysterious, don't you think?" Alison asked Antony.

"Well, I believe that love and affection are two very different things."

"I don't think we really understand how love works or where it comes from."

She studied his heavily stubbled face.

"I think that people enter relationships with unclear expectations and unbalanced levels of commitment."

"I guess if you really love somebody, you are prepared to accept their flaws."

She could feel the tears brewing.

"I think it's all about an initial connection and then seeing where that leads to."

"I'm not sleeping very well in this place. I've a lot to tell you, but I really don't know where to start," she said.

"Well, it's certainly some sort of predicament you've got yourself into."

"I've felt so alone here. You've no idea how much it means to me that you've come to visit."

"I think you need to put me straight here … explain everything that's happened."

"I'm in so much trouble."

"Well, talk to me. You know you can trust me."

"Do I look a terrible mess? I bet I look awful, don't I?"

Antony laughed.

"Well, I don't suppose you can get your hair and nails done very often, in here."

Alison's mind started with its negative self-talk … the bad emotions were starting. She mustered as much control as she could to try and keep them under control. Her anxiety was taking over.

A flash of light from across the room distracted her.

"Should I start back in my childhood? Tell you about my abuse?"

She studied her bare feet … her naked toes.

She rose from her chair and performed some ballet steps.

"This is how I danced when I was a small child."

Her eyes teared.

"So how much have they told you about what happened?"

"Just that you've not been your best self, and that you are here because you attacked a woman."

"I didn't mean to ... attack her, I mean."

"I'm really worried about you. I wish I knew how to help you."

He appeared flustered.

"Are you nervous ... being in here on your own with me?"

"No, I'm just trying to keep my emotions under control. It's so sad to see you in here like this."

"Do you think it's okay that I attacked her in self-defence?"

"To a certain degree, yes. I understand that you experience the world in a different way to the average person."

"You mean like I thought that she was out to get me, and that she was trying to control my world?"

"I believe the world is a dangerous place for you, and that you are extremely vulnerable."

"Dr. Horne is helping me … and Dr. Eliott, too … but I prefer Dr. Horne."

Alison moved towards him and rested her head on his shoulder. In return, he ruffled her hair, which she found incredibly endearing. She moved her right hand to the top of his thigh. He gazed into her eyes, and she gazed back into his.

"I so wish I wasn't locked up in here," she said.

"I'm going to help you. I want you out of here as soon as possible."

His brows were stitched with concern.

Alison smiled.

"That's easy for you to say, but I don't know how that's possible when my whole world is sliding into the mouth of hell."

"Well, I have your back, and I'm going to do all I can to help you."

"My mother tortured me, and my Father was a monster. I've discovered this during my sessions with Dr. Horne and Dr. Eliott," she said, her voice full of fury.

"We're not going to lose this fight."

The door opened and a nurse lingered in the doorway.

"I'm sorry to break this up, but it's time, I'm afraid."

Antony moved over and kissed Alison on the forehead. She looked up at him.

"I'll wait for you to come and rescue me."

Back in her room, Alison closed her eyes and thought back to the day of the attack, the day her life had changed forever. Dr. Horne opened her bedroom door and stepped in.

"Antony kissed me on my forehead when he left. But kissing me is wrong, because I'm not well enough to have a relationship, not with all of my medical issues. I don't understand why he would want to get involved with me under the circumstances. To be honest, I don't know much about Antony."

"Where did you meet him?" Dr. Horne asked.

"He lives in Bournemouth. That's where I met him."

She experienced a faint sort of sadness, which changed into an excruciating emotional pain.

At that very moment, she was back in the

Jacuzzi, the very first time she had met Antony. Everything was off-balance.

Was she in love? It was as though all that seemed to matter to her now was Antony.

A dark figure surfaced in front of her eyes. It spoke.

"I'm a peaceful soul. I'm not here to pick a fight."

It hovered over Alison.

"I died in 1924. A painful death … my head was severed."

Its face became clear, contorted in a broad, toothless grin.

Alison was aware that Dr. Horne was watching her, so she plastered an expression on her own face, which resulted in a fixed, creepy smirk.

Her eyes were drawn back to the dark figure's face as it let out a blood-curdling scream.

In response, Alison retorted with a panicked cry, shrill and urgent.

Chapter 16

Alison stared blankly at Dr. Horne.

"When I was 16, my Dad's friend raped me in the basement of our home. He stunk of beer. That's all I could think about ... the same smell as my Dad. He pushed me to the floor and asked me to have sex. He tried to persuade me at first, whilst he groped at my clothes. He promised to be gentle, telling me he knew I was a virgin. He said he'd seen the way I'd looked at him ever since I was a child, and he'd waited until I'd turned 16 to make it more respectable. I told him no ... that I didn't want to have sex with him. I kicked myself free, but he followed me and tackled me to the floor once more. After that, everything became foggy.

"As he entered me, I heard him say, 'There! I've popped your cherry!'. I wanted to die at that very moment. I've never told a soul until now. I'm so ashamed. My panic attacks became worse straight after it happened.

"The next day, I cut myself for the first time. After that, I didn't care who I had sex with. It no longer mattered. I was no longer a virgin. I started drinking alcohol to try and block it all out.

"You have to understand, there was nothing I could have done to stop him; he was huge. I remember the way he smiled at me when he said those terrible words about my cherry. The carpet in the basement was red … red for danger … red for stop … but he didn't stop. Twice more, he raped me, after that night … even made me have oral sex."

"Didn't you even tell your mother?"

"I couldn't. She wouldn't have believed me, anyway."

"I've some books I'd like to give you to read, to help you overcome this terrible act of abuse towards you. There is no quick fix to all that has happened to you but being able to voice what happened is a very good start."

"Do you think it's too late for me to seek justice for what others have done to me?"

"Well, it would be very tough to prove anything at this late stage."

"If I could sue him and get some money, I

could open my flower restaurant."

"With great respect, Alison, I don't think it works like that."

"It's no wonder I've not amounted to much in life, is it really?"

"Well, it's certainly not a pretty past, Alison, but as I've said before you can change things for your future."

Later, in the early evening, Alison was moved back to the main ward and was relieved to find that she was to be placed back in her old room with Carina. They sat in silence as they ate their dinner.

Afterwards, Carina pushed her plate to one side.

"How's the baby doing?"

"I'm scared. I'm so stupid and selfish," Alison said.

A grating alarm signalled it was time for their doors to be closed for the night.

"Have you thought of any names for the baby yet?" Carina asked.

"Yeah, I want something unusual, not boring like Alison. Maybe Birdie or Mickey. I don't know if it's a boy or a girl yet."

"Yeah, I like my name, Carina, 'cos it's

different. What about Violet or Skye?"

"Antony might want me to call the baby by his name. He came to see me, you know."

"Really? How exciting! Was it romantic?"

"I know it sounds improbable in this place, but, yes, it was."

"How? What did he say? Is he excited about the baby?"

Alison picked at the cuticles on her nails and yawned, unable to prevent the lie from leaving her mouth.

"He asked me to marry him."

"Oh! No way! That's so exciting!"

Carina dived off her bed and hugged Alison. Squirming, Alison pulled away.

"Careful! You'll squash the baby."

She was frustrated with herself for having lied to her so-called friend.

"You know this could work out perfectly for you. The hospital will be more sympathetic knowing you are pregnant. But if Antony was prepared to say he was going to marry you and help look after you and the baby, that's got to be in your favour."

At that moment, Alison despised herself. Why had she told such lies?

"I feel really tired now. I need to get some sleep."

She lay on her bed and no sooner than she did so, a male voice started in her head. This time it was different. The voice told her that he loved her and to keep moving on with her life, that she was going in the right direction, getting the help she needed particularly from Dr. Horne. He told her she was insane, but things were going to become good in the future. She closed her eyes and drifted off to sleep, feeling comforted.

During the night she was woken by a high-pitched wailing. Red orbs danced across the walls in the darkness. Standing before her were two people she'd never seen before: a woman and a man. Alison lifted her pillow, placed it over her head and closed her eyes.

Trying to forget all that was going on around her, she began to dream about her restaurant. People would travel from far away to eat there. It would be warm, hospitable and elegant, with great food ... cosy, and full of flowers.

A vague awareness that something was wrong startled her from her dream.

Carina was in Alison's bed, her strong arms wrapped around her, a hug stronger than anything she'd ever known. The world stopped still on its axis.

"Hey," Carina whispered.

Her sexual connotations were clear. The kisses on her neck turned into gentle bites. Her lips moved further down towards her breasts.

Alison was lost in a labyrinth of confusion; she could feel her cheeks blushing. Carina's lips were hot and seductive as she bit and licked her breasts. Alison was nervous and uneasy, but she couldn't resist her as she rubbed her own breasts into hers. Sexually, she was on point, turning her on. She smelled good … female and lovely. Alison arched her back, responding, touching Carina's breasts. A woman was seducing her, and it felt good. Wow!

The following morning, Alison watched Carina as she exercised in their room.

"Come on, Alison. Join me. We need to keep fit in this place, pregnant or not."

Joining her in some stretches, Alison thought about what had occurred during the night and was full of guilt about the lies she'd told about Antony being the father of her baby, and that he'd asked her to marry him. What a mess, her life had become. She felt crushed, full of uncertainty, as if she were drowning.

"How come you can be so patient and so kind, Carina?"

"I make a lot of effort, that's why. I've been here a long time and I'm ready to get out of here now ... make my own way in life."

"I know! I'm ready now, I think, to start taking responsibility for my own actions."

"We've a strong connection, you and I," Carina said.

"I want to be just like you," Alison said.

"No, you don't," Carina laughed. "I haven't got it all together just yet. I still have my crazy moments."

"I want to be the best mother possible to this baby."

Alison rubbed her hand over her tummy.

"Well, you can count on me to help you as much as possible through this pregnancy."

"That's wonderful to know, Carina. Thank you so much."

"I've changed for the better in here. You can as well, you know."

"The biggest challenge I'm currently facing is getting my emotions under control."

"I've found it helps to start each day as a fresh one and try to start off with an upbeat attitude."

Carina looked into Alison's eyes. Alison

didn't understand why, but she almost felt blissful. She now understood how to make herself feel happier. She just needed to short-circuit the negativity in her brain and focus purely on the positives. Her trust towards Carina was increasing, and she felt an intense loyalty towards her. They had experienced a beautiful, intimate, human bond together. The warmth from the 'cuddling' was beyond anything she had ever known.

After breakfast, she calmly walked alongside the nurse, Leta, towards Dr. Horne's office, but in her mind, she was meeting with her lawyer.

His enthusiasm was the first thing to strike her. It was more than she had prepared herself for. There was a downright unpleasant aura around him. She listened as he laid out different scenarios before her. Mid-to-late fifties, she guessed his age to be.

"It would be easy for you to play the victim here and reverse the roles."

She stopped him.

"No. I don't want to go down that route. I want to take responsibility for my actions."

"Well, you could plead guilty with diminished responsibility. I feel you certainly have a case for this. The attack was not only in self-defence, but also driven by a primitive human emotion. You reacted physically to an outburst directed towards you; a survival mechanism kicked in ... basically, the fight or flight response. Without any pre-thought, your mind told your body to fight. We can make a case that this emotional response came from a highly personalised reaction. The mind is incredibly complex and yours can certainly be medically explained as such. Repeated exposure to abuse during your childhood can be used to explain why your response may have been so violent without intent to harm ... a form of desensitisation."

Chapter 17

Alison studied her lawyer's face as he spoke; he was certainly handsome for his age.

"So what's the story with the husband of the woman you attacked? What was his name? Darren Marlowe? Did you have a fling with him?" he asked.

"Yeah! Classic affair with a married man. You know how it goes," she replied.

"And you met this man face-to-face, not over the internet?"

"Yes. Initially he made me feel special. I was lonely, you know, but my triumph soon turned to despair, when I realised that he'd lied to me, and that he still loved his wife," Alison replied, stone-faced.

"And as a result of the attack on his wife, you have ended up in this 20-inmate unit, full of other women who have committed crimes believed to have been carried out due to different mental health problems?"

"Yeah. It's pretty horrific being locked up in here, but I guess it's better than being in prison … and I like my roommate."

"Have you been allowed to see any friends or relatives from outside while you've been here?"

"Yes. My friend Antony has been to visit. I don't have any relatives, and I don't have many friends either."

She jumped up from her chair and began to pace back and forth across the room. Her lawyer gave her a weird look.

"Why are you pacing?"

"I'm bored!" she replied. "I thought seeing you would be a lot more interesting, and now you've triggered my vivid mental imagery."

"Are they medicating you here?" he asked.

"Yes. It's supposed to help with the voices and stuff, but it doesn't really help. They don't stop. Anyway, thinking is hard work."

"Do you think it was a stupid thing you did … to try and run away?"

"My whole life has been blighted with stupidity. I don't know why, but I'm in a deeply sombre mood. I thought you were supposed to offer me comfort and support."

She felt the electricity in the room change.

"Well, I'm here as your lawyer, to represent you, to work together and try to build some kind of relationship with you."

"What would you say if you knew I was pregnant? That Darren Marlowe is the father of this baby?"

"Is this a hypothetical question, or is this for real?"

"It's for real. What type of ethical dilemma does that put you in?"

"Well, it provides me with a whole new train of thought."

"By the way, you haven't even told me your name. What am I supposed to call you?"

"I'm Barry Lanson."

"Well, being trapped in this place is the pits, Barry. I love to be outside. I love nature and flowers. One day, I'm going to own a flower restaurant."

"Cabin fever, they call it … in a clinical sense," Barry said.

"It makes me feel angry, being stuck in here."

"But you've kept that under control. You've not harmed anyone whilst you've been in here.

"Now, going back to the pregnancy, would you be willing for me to request that Darren Marlowe provide a DNA test? It could strengthen your case immensely if he *is* the father of your unborn baby. I also need to examine your arrest sheet and assess how much police pressure was put upon you."

"I met him – Darren – on a bench in Bournemouth."

"Then what happened?"

"He took me for a very expensive dinner the following evening, with lots of red wine."

"How did he persuade you?"

"I guess I was lonely."

"I think it will be easy for me to paint him in a bad light."

"What about the demons in my head?"

"You are vulnerable and stressed, Alison, which won't help. Continue to work with the doctor's here. I'm sure they're helping you with your issues."

"But where do they come from? Why do I see them? Why do I hear them?"

"Well, no one enters adulthood unscarred, but unfortunately, your past relationship with your parents has left you more scarred than most. I'm not a doctor, I'm a lawyer, but I see this a lot in my line of work."

The same night, Alison was wide awake at 3am, replaying her visit with her lawyer in her mind. Her thoughts turned to Carina and how hurt she appeared to have been by Alison's meeting with her lawyer. She had blatantly snubbed her and didn't wish to discuss it, as she was "too tired and needed space to think about her own issues".

Curling up in a ball in her bed, Alison began to cry like a baby, reeling with anxiety. Frustrated, she punched the wall at the side of her bed. Her mind was becoming more chaotic and confused. She couldn't fathom why Carina had been so uncaring towards her. Unable to withstand it any longer, she decided to wake Carina up to discuss her feelings. After her earlier mood, though, it was hardly surprising that Carina's reaction to being woken up in the middle of the night was to scream at her.

"For Christ's sake, Alison, just leave me alone! I told you I needed space to sort out my own issues. It's taken me all night to fall asleep, and now you've gone and bloody well woken me up! The sex between us was fantasy, nothing more. It's not bloody reality; nothing in this place is. I was just fulfilling a desire with you. Don't go bloody well getting attached to me. I can't deal with it."

The following morning, still seething at Carina's words, and not having spoken to her since, it was time in Alison's mind to go for her ultrasound scan. The sonographer asked her to lie on the couch where she applied a gel onto her tummy, having tucked tissue paper around her clothing to protect it. She then passed a probe over her skin, and as if by magic, a black and white picture of Alison's baby appeared on the screen of the ultrasound machine.

"I estimate you to be 14 weeks pregnant," the sonographer said. "The baby is growing normally, with no obvious abnormalities."

Staring at her baby on the screen, Alison thought about how she could have lost hope in life. How had her whole life collapsed around her, when there was new life growing inside of her? Why had so many things gone wrong, and yet she'd managed to get this right? How had she ended up in this deep, dark, downward spiral? Was it possible to bounce back for the sake of this baby? She wanted to give the baby the best life possible, one free from hurt, abuse and pain, but was she capable of doing that? She had never wanted anything so badly in her life. It was time to recognise her own value. She was going to be a mother.

She needed to find ways to allow her mental

A PARALLEL PERSONA

and physical wellbeing to heal and prepare for the forthcoming birth. On her return to her room, she was relieved to discover that Carina had gone to the common room for some therapy, and she revelled in the quietness. She grabbed one of the books Dr. Horne had given her and snuggled into her bed to read. The book jolted memories from her childhood and teenage years.

Rubbing her hand over her tummy, she said, "I love you, baby."

Her thoughts drifted to flowers, with pleasing images of spring wildflowers blooming in her restaurant.

A knock at her door startled her. Dr. Horne stood in the doorway.

"How would you like me to take you shopping this afternoon? We could get you some new clothes. I am going to have to put a lot of trust in you that you'll behave and not do anything stupid, though."

"Oh, I won't! I promise! I'm never going to put my baby at risk ever again."

"Alison, there is no baby."

The afternoon was wonderful. Just being outside in the fresh air lifted Alison's spirits, as she and Dr. Horne wandered around the shops in the town centre. Dr. Horne even took her for lunch in a lovely restaurant, and afterwards they purchased several outfits from H&M, her favourite being a black and white dress, which she decided she would save to wear for Antony's next visit … if he were to decide to come again.

Chapter 18

Putting on one of the outfits she'd purchased with Dr. Horne the day before, Alison felt more positive than she had in a long time. Today was a fresh start, time to try and understand herself better. It was time for growth, development and change. She would examine the past, but leave it there, in the past, where it belonged. Bad times could end, and she felt determined to stop them from happening in the future. In the hospital, she'd realised that she had an opportunity for their therapies and self-care practices to help her get well, to feel at peace with herself.

An excitement at the prospect was brewing within her. No more mistakes. This was her chance to safeguard her baby's and her own future. She could turn this mess around. It was as though the baby had caused a penny to drop in her mind. She would leave all this nonsense and horror behind her. She would dig herself out of the hole she'd dug herself into. She could change, and she would. Her life could turn out to be so different.

She didn't know why, but she began to laugh out loud. Change, but in small steps, that's what she'd do. A weird glow surrounded her. Instead of rejecting it or being fearful of it, she decided to sit on her bed and just observe it. She knew what she could see was absurd, but she also knew it was real. She was ready to move away from her mental darkness. The irrational part of her brain needed to be left behind. 'Hell on earth' was no longer going to be her mantra. After all, wasn't everybody a little crazy? She just needed to rein in her craziness, just like everyone else did.

Alison's life had certainly been turned inside out. Survival of her baby was now her paramount concern. She was prepared to put one step forward at a time. Her baby would not suffer the way she had. She could get through this. She was not alone. She would make sure she summoned the strength and courage to face each new day positively. She would heal her heart. She would make her way onto solid ground.

With this mind-set, Alison joined in the morning group session with Dr. Horne. She smiled pleasantly at Janet, the woman she'd previously despised, and she nodded in acknowledgement at Carina, having taken the empty seat next to her. Three other women she didn't recognise completed the circle.

Dr. Horne opened the session.

"Today, we are going to discuss how growing up with a difficult parent can affect our behaviour as adults."

Janet spoke first.

"There's no such thing as a perfect parent though, is there?"

Carina said, "Yeah! But there's good enough, and then there's just downright horrid, isn't there?"

"Some parents are just cruel," the blonde lady said.

"We can move on, though. We don't have to be the same as them," Alison said.

"Absolutely, Alison. That's the whole point. We can't change what's been done to us, but we can change things in our lives from now on," Dr. Horne said.

"My dad killed five people. Just walked into a bank and randomly shot them. All women! He hated women. I was twelve. Imagine your whole world rocked by something like that. How do you even begin to fathom that one out?" Janet asked.

"That must have been awful for you. Well, I've made my mind up, and I'm going to change my future. I'm going to try and see life from a different perspective, not just what my past has taught me," Alison said.

"That's great, Alison. This is something we can all grasp. Sometimes, it can feel confusing to let go of your cruel pasts and rebalance the future," Dr. Horne said.

"Some of you may not have experienced love from your parents, but this does not mean you aren't capable of self-love, loving others, and receiving love. We can start this process by being brutally honest with ourselves. It's okay to show one another our vulnerabilities," she continued.

Alison sniffed the palm of her right hand as an alarm bell in her brain attracted her attention.

"Janet, are you seriously contemplating taking your own life at the first opportunity?" Alison asked.

"I just want my pain to end," Janet cried. "How do you know I feel that way?"

Looking around the room, slightly embarrassed, Alison said, "Because I think I've finally worked it out. The voices I hear and the things I see are spirits talking to me and guiding me. I just need to learn to control it and not to fear it. All my life, I've been told I'm crazy, but I'm slowly starting to figure it all out. I now believe I've been given a gift. I just need to learn how to use it properly."

Dr. Horne allowed the conversation to continue, sitting back in her chair quietly and observing.

"That's amazing. Don't you all have days where everything is just so dark?" Janet asked.

"Yes, when everything is crashing down on you," Carina said.

"Disappointment! I'm just so disappointed with how my life has turned out that my patience with everything just runs out," the blonde lady said.

"No sense of peace," Janet said.

"No plans to look forward to," Carina said.

"A failure! That's what I am," the blonde lady said.

"On your own … no one understands you," Janet said.

"You want to give up, run away, stay in bed, get off this stupid planet," Carina said.

"The darkness and despair are never ending,"

the blonde lady said.

Interrupting, Dr. Horne said, "Well, this has opened up a very useful conversation. Thank you, Alison, for your input today. It has been most helpful for everybody to say how they feel and to try and listen and understand one another. All I can say to you all is, with help and therapy, these dark thoughts can pass. There is a light at the end of that dark tunnel. Today's session is over, so you are all dismissed. Alison, I would like to see you for a solo therapy session in 30 minutes."

Alison took the chair opposite Dr. Horne. Dr. Horne spoke first.

"I watched what you did today with Janet. I've been giving some serious thought to the voices you hear and the things you see. Can you explain a bit more to me, now that you seem to be on a much more stable path."

"Well, I've realised that I am actually communicating with spirits. The voices aren't just in my head, and when I see them, they're not in my imagination. I get premonitions too. I often know when things are going to happen … not just personal stuff, catastrophic world events, too. I see angels, but I've been living in fear of the demons. I think my fear is what has attracted them. I'm going to try and overcome that, so that they no longer come to me. I'm very susceptible to energies, which is something else I need to learn to control."

"It seems that the task of separating good thoughts from silly ones is extremely hard for you, Alison. I'm not sure how much you live in a narrative you've woven for yourself. But what you're saying makes me worry that I may be wrong. I'm suspicious in my own mind about a spirit world that's able to communicate to people in this way," Dr. Horne replied.

The air in the room went cold. Alison felt dizzy. She stared at her feet. Sadness swept over her, and she shivered. The floor begun to vibrate. She could feel breathing against her ear.

She wanted to interrupt Dr. Horne and explain what was happening, but instead she glanced at her watch, wishing the session was over and she could return to the sanctuary of her own room. It seemed pointless trying to explain any further.

Dr. Horne was still talking, but Alison had given up trying to listen. She obviously thought Alison's experiences were some type of sick joke. There was no point attempting to share her point of view. It was better if she just kept it all to herself. The rest of the session was torture for her, and as it ended, she rushed back to her room as fast as she could.

On opening the door, though, Alison was disappointed to find Carina lying on her bed. She could feel the tears brewing, but didn't want to cry in front of Carina. She gave herself a hard pinch to try and prevent herself from doing so.

Carina stared at Alison.

"I can't take anymore."

"The mood I'm in, I really don't give a fuck," Alison replied.

"This place is crazy. We're all crazy. The problem is, you never get used to it," Carina continued, choosing to ignore Alison's comment.

"Didn't you hear me the first time? I don't give a fuck."

Remaining silent, Carina rolled over and turned her back on Alison.

"You're such an asshole, Carina. I wish I didn't have to share a room with you."

Alison didn't know why, but she began to laugh out loud. At least, it seemed to be calming her mind.

Lights out came around quickly, and before she knew it, it was bedtime. Unable to sleep, she tossed and turned, her mind churning. Desperate to enter Dreamland, she tugged at her hair. She reached for the glass of water on her bedside cabinet and took a few gulps.

More and more confusion clouded her thoughts. The room was always warm, but tonight it seemed uncomfortably hot, and she was sweating buckets. She punched her pillow, with frustration.

Chapter 19

The following day, Alison found herself sitting opposite her lawyer, Barry Lanson.

"I know this is an unscheduled meeting, Alison, but I wanted to speak with you regarding the unborn baby and Darren Marlowe. I wrote to him explaining your claim that he is the father of the child. He called me immediately after he received the letter. He was in quite a state of shock and extremely concerned about his wife discovering your claim.

"I might add that she is to be discharged from hospital in the near future; she appears to be recovering well from her injuries. His initial reaction was one of denial … that it's impossible for you to be pregnant with his baby. He then changed tack and asked if it would be possible for it to be kept secret. I informed him that that would be impossible, at which point, he became quite angry. I explained about the DNA testing."

"Yeah, he's hardly my knight in shining armour, is he?"

"Well, if we do prove that he is the father, he will need to take financial responsibility for the baby," Barry said.

Alison nodded and frowned.

Barry rose from his chair, satisfied that Alison had understood the full implications of the situation she now found herself in.

"I'll be in touch soon. Take care of yourself … and that baby."

Dr. Eliott entered the room.

"How are you holding up, Alison?"

She took the seat the lawyer had vacated.

"What do you care?"

Alison's eyes narrowed.

"I've a letter for you," Dr. Eliott said, passing it across the desk.

Tearing it open, Alison read the words to herself. Her face lit up as she realised it was from Antony. He told her how worried he was about her and asked if there was anything she needed. He said that he was trying to arrange a visit as soon as he possibly could.

It was everything she'd hoped for in that it confirmed he wanted to see her again. She looked over at Dr. Eliott.

"It's from Antony, my boyfriend. He's coming to visit again. I'm going to figure everything out and make a good life for my baby."

The buzz from Dr. Eliott's bleeper broke up the meeting.

"Sorry, Alison. I have an emergency."

Placing a hand on her stomach, Alison spoke to her baby.

"He's coming to see us. Everything's going to be okay."

Back in her room, relieved that Carina was off doing something else, Alison sat on her bed and ran her fingers along the wall.

Brick walls!

There for a reason!

Keeping her penned in to sort out her mind!

In her thoughts, she started to list all the challenges she needed to overcome. Finally, her brain seemed to be functioning fairly rationally most of the time. She was aware that her future was going to be tough, but she was determined to make it right, both for herself and for the baby.

A still calmness overcame her. She no longer felt torn or confused. She would solve all of this and make things better. She could do this. She had to. She wouldn't give up. She would keep going, no matter what. Antony would help her. She couldn't wait to see him.

Alison didn't know why, but she started to cry. She would not allow her inner demons to haunt her again.

Silence fell around her … peace … as she allowed the room to feel her pain.

A ringing phone broke her solitude, but she had no phone. A young woman appeared standing by the side of her bed.

This time, feeling no fear, Alison asked, "Who are you?"

The woman held out her hand.

"It's all right," she said.

"But who are you?" Alison asked.

The woman's blue eyes opened wide.

"You need to unlearn what you've learned since childhood."

She smiled gently.

Feeling calm and collected, Alison smiled back at the young woman. Her anger and frustration seemed to just melt away. The figure vanished as quickly as she'd appeared. Alison chose one of the books that Dr. Horne had provided her with, lay back on her bed and began to read about how to make changes and move forward with your life.

Her thoughts drifted to Darren and his wife, and how she might take the news of the pregnancy.

Why had she believed his lies ... his falsehoods? Why did her hatred run so deep towards his wife? Was it just sheer frustration with not being able to be with him after all the promises he'd made her? Was it all part of her psychological disorder?

How would Darren feel about the innocent little life growing inside her? Would he always see her as some crazy woman he once got involved with?

What if he wanted visiting rights, or tried to take the baby away to live with them?

Chapter 20

After taking a shower, Alison towel-dried her wet hair and then brushed out the knots, leaving it to dry by itself. She brushed her teeth and flossed. She picked out the dress she'd been saving for Antony's visit; she still couldn't believe she was to see him this morning. She clipped her toenails and put on a pair of flip-flops.

The hug Antony greeted her with meant more to her than any words he could have said. It was a tight, strong, loving, breath-taking embrace, which immediately made her feel safe.

"You look great, Alison … much better than you did when I last saw you," he said.

"I am. Dr. Horne has given me special permission for us to walk in the grounds, and because I've been doing so well, she has said I'm allowed extra visiting time with you today.

C'mon. I'll show you the gardens. They're beautiful."

Alison led the way through the corridor and one of the nurses keyed in the password to open the doors, which opened out on to the path between the rosebushes. Alison took his hand.

"I work in the laundry for a couple of hours a day now, and I'm feeling so much better."

Antony's voice was relaxed, soft and calm.

"Well, I can certainly see a change for the better."

"Thank you," she said, admiring his casual clothes and athletic frame. As always, the floral and woody smells of the gardens lifted her mood even higher. Everything felt so romantic.

She knew in her heart that it was imperative to tell him about her pregnancy, but a knot of anxiety registered with her ... a sense of unease. Would he be happy for her, or distressed by the thought of it? Her mind went blank; she didn't want to ruin her special time in the gardens with him. Her stomach began to churn, and a tingling sensation in her head was beginning to make her feel as if she might faint. Maybe it was a bad idea to tell him? She had to stop this vicious circle of thoughts before it ruined the morning. Could she trust him not to judge her? Would he continue to be supportive?

"It's great to see you, Alison. I would have come back sooner, but I've been working abroad."

Alison relaxed a little. She just needed to be herself … nothing more, nothing less.

"I'm scared for your future. Have you heard any more about your trial?"

"They've said it takes time. It may be a few weeks yet."

"I'll come back sooner next time. I've no plans to work away again for a while."

She squeezed his hand.

"Aren't these gardens beautiful? I wish I could be out here all the time."

"I like spending time with you. I just wish the circumstances were different. It doesn't put me off though. I still want to get to know you better, and hopefully you'll be out of here sooner than you think."

"My therapy is going well. I'm more in control of my life than I've ever been. I've more sense of self. I really feel as though I am coming into my own. I'm much calmer and more at peace.

"Look! Here's the herb garden. I love the smell of herbs. I will have my flower restaurant one day." She bent down to smell the lavender. "I'll use the flowers and leaves in salads, dressings and desserts."

She moved further along. "This is thyme. You have to use this sparingly as the flavour can be overpowering."

She carried on touching and naming all of the different herbs: mint, basil, sage, rosemary and chives.

Antony picked a flower and handed it to her.

"For you."

Beaming, she asked, "How did you know it was my favourite?"

The flower fell to the floor. Antony was no longer standing in front of her and had transformed into the figure of Dr. Horne.

An ominous, mysterious, droning siren buzzed in Alison's ears.

Shocked, she looked down and focused on her slippers. Slippers? She'd been wearing flip-flops, hadn't she? She stared blankly at Dr. Horne.

As she stood there, it was as though she was living two lives. But which one was the truth? Her head certainly wasn't clear. Starting to wobble, she sat down on the garden path. Her brain was overwhelmed as she observed everything around her. She felt lost and powerless.

Wanting to speak, she moved her lips, but no sound escaped from them.

Dreams, visions, memories and thoughts!

She had no idea of what was real and what was not.

She stroked her tummy, feeling for the curve of her pregnancy, but her tummy was flat.

Her mouth opened wide, and this time her cry rose high into the air, imploring the world to swallow her and remove her pain.

Dr. Horne sat down beside Alison on the path and held both of her hands with her own.

"It's okay! Let it out. Do you remember your name and where you are?"

"Yes. My name is Erica Goodman, and I'm in a rehabilitation hospital, and you are Dr. Horne. I'm here because I have a head injury from being involved in a car accident. My husband was killed outright."

"Do you remember how long you've been here?"

"Yes. Five years. That day was the worst day

of my life."

"The pain, shock and heartbreak all cause you to drift off into an imaginary life. I'm afraid you had a relapse; it all happened again," Dr. Horne said.

"So, I'm not pregnant, am I? There is no Darren Marlowe. He doesn't exist. There's no Antony either. I've not attacked anyone. I'm not facing trial for anything. My parents are dead though, aren't they?"

"Yes, that's all true. C'mon. Let me help you up, and we'll head back down the path and go inside. It's getting rather chilly out here," Dr. Horne said.

"I don't understand. I don't know why this happens. Why do I live an imaginary life inside my head, and then I wake up from it, and everything has to sink in all over again?"

"It's okay. I know you feel angry about it, and that's fine. One day, you will stop doing this, and you will remain in the reality of your situation for the rest of your life," Dr. Horne said.

"I just get so lost and stuck. The whole world carries on as if nothing has changed, but it can never be the same again."

"Your brain lies to you, and your imagination convinces you that you are leading a completely different life," Dr. Horne said.

"Is there any hope that I can function in reality only, one day?"

Back in the safety of her room, realising now that there was no Carina, her mind felt calm and yet chaotic. She recalled waking up from a coma. Six weeks, they told her, she'd been asleep.

Afterwards, she had to come to terms with so much trauma: the news of her husband's passing … having to learn to walk again … being able to hear what people were saying but not being able to make sense of their words, almost as if they were speaking in a foreign language. Her speech had been affected too, but she had slowly learned to form words again over the following months. When she'd enquired if she had any children, she was grateful that the answer had been a negative one. At least that meant that no one else was suffering like she was.

Each time she resurfaced like this, she would experience the terrible grief around her husband's death as if it was the first time she'd been given the news. She wondered if she would ever be well enough to leave the hospital, to function normally, to build her life once more?

That night, she slept restlessly but remained in the reality of who she was: Erica Goodman, 38 years old, who had suffered a traumatic head injury five years previously. The next day, she attended a yoga session, where she remembered some of the long-term patients, who greeted her warmly and stated that they were pleased to see her feeling well again. She took her lunch with a couple of the patients she remembered and chatted to them about their own progress and families. In the afternoon, she selected a fiction novel from the library and took a comfortable armchair in the sitting room overlooking the gardens. Some of the patients who drifted around, she didn't recognise, and she wondered if they were new or if she'd just forgotten who they were. After dinner, she retired to her bedroom and listened to music on the radio.

The following morning, Erica studied her reflection in the mirror. The angles to her face were thinner than she remembered. It was strange to be able to see her own image once more, and not that of Alison, the woman she had conjured up in her mind.

She ran her fingers over the smooth surface of the mirror, reaching out to her own reflection. Her skin was shiny, so she dabbed some powder over her nose and cheeks. She added further make-up and created a colourful effect on her eyelids. Now, the image staring back at her looked more like the Erica she knew.

Sitting informally with Dr. Horne on a bench in the gardens, they discussed Erica's recent decline into her imaginary world.

"This time you've been gone for approximately three months. It's been one of your worst episodes since your very first one. What do you think causes it, Erica?"

"I suppose it's because I seek comfort by not having to face my reality."

Dr. Horne smiled.

"It's not as if you even give yourself an easy ride in your imaginary life. This time, it was particularly horrific for you."

"Yeah. It's as though I still want to hurt, but not with my own truth," Erica said.

"I've seen it before – seeking distraction to get away from the real stuff – but this is on a level I've never experienced before during any of my 20 odd years of working in this field."

"At the time, anything seems better than the truth," Erica said.

"I understand that the truth is scary, but you have to face it in order to move on."

"I know. I do understand that I need to take responsibility and detach myself from these fantasy worlds that I create," Erica said.

"You need to work towards a place that resonates with you. Even this time, you never gave up on the dream of owning your flower restaurant. It's the one thing, which always remains in place. One dream you never let go of."

"I know it's time to face the music, however much it hurts," Erica said.

"Only you can do this. You need to forgive yourself. I know you were driving at the time, but it's been proven that the accident was not your fault."

"Have Frank or Laurence been to see me this time?"

"No. We refused their visits. You've not been well enough. But if you like, I'll notify them you can receive visitors again now. Or would you prefer to contact them yourself? I need to sort out your phone. You're well enough to have that back now."

"Am I allowed to walk in the gardens on my own again?"

"Yes. The gardens have always been good for you."

"Yeah. My time outside is much more than just a breath of fresh air to me."

Chapter 21

As she wandered in the gardens, her memories of Bryan flooded back. Their last trip together had been to Prague, where they'd admired the alluring architecture, drunk abundant amounts of beer and enjoyed a thoroughly romantic week together. They'd spent one particularly memorable evening at the historic Prague State Opera. One morning they'd got lost in the peaceful and elegant Jewish Quarter. They'd window-shopped along the Parizska, admiring the luxurious clothes and other items in the shop windows, and then taken a long, wine-filled lunch in Old Town Square. They'd strolled along the river and shopped for glass and porcelain. He had bought her an exquisite aquamarine necklace with matching earrings. They'd stumbled across a classical concert inside St. Nicholas Church.

He'd spoiled her rotten on that trip, and they'd stayed in a fabulous five-star hotel. It had been spring, two months before the accident – a time when the sun had shone in her world. She smiled to herself as she recalled his attempts at trying out some Czech words from his guidebook with the waiters.

The memories of her home flooded back – their magnificent top floor apartment in the central area of Bournemouth. They'd decorated it with love and had been so immensely proud of what they'd achieved: the minimalist décor, designer lighting, vintage furnishings and the contemporary art, which adorned the walls. Two years, it had taken them to achieve the look they'd desired. Her thoughts drifted to the roof top terrace, where they'd spent many an evening, drinking wine and chatting.

She traced her finger along the scar on the lower inside part of her right arm: a permanent reminder of the fateful accident. She would call Frank, her older brother, later today, once she'd retrieved her phone from Dr. Horne.

Her mind raced back to her old life: her old school, her classroom, the children she'd taught. She'd always called them *her* children. Hatty Arnold was her favourite out of the last class of five-year-olds she'd had the pleasure of teaching. But although she'd enjoyed it, she had always dreamed of owning her own restaurant and had started to put plans into place a month before the fateful day.

It was to be an upmarket restaurant, located in Bournemouth, offering full table service, focusing on the quality of the cuisine and affording a floral ambience. Her aim was to provide her patrons with a delightful dining experience. Her idea had been to run the front of house herself, playing the role of the elegant host, and to employ a talented chef and kitchen staff. She had begun to make a business plan and had started to think about menus and pricing. She had a decent amount of start-up capital from an inheritance left to her by her aunt, who had passed away the previous year. *'Gosh!'* the thought struck her. *'Was that really six years ago?'*

She had located a restaurant and had viewed it with the potential to buy it only a week before the accident. A tear rolled down her cheek as she recalled how excited she'd been, and how Bryan was going to attend the second viewing with her, but the accident occurred on the day before that should have happened. She had even mapped out in her head, how she would change the layout and design to maximise the effect she hoped to achieve with the flowers.

Returning to her room, she was pleased to see

her phone on the bedside cabinet. Now, she could call Frank. He must have been so worried about her. Three months she'd lived in that other state. *'What nonsense,'* she told herself.

Nervously, she dialled his number. Frank picked up on the third ring.

"Sis! Is that you, Erica?"

Erica began to sob.

"Yes, Frank. It's me."

"Oh, my God! I've been out of my mind with worry about you. Are you okay? Dr. Horne's been in regular contact with me, but she said you'd had a real bad time of it, this time. She advised against me visiting."

"I know. I'm okay. She says you can visit now. Can you come soon?"

"Of course, love. I'll come tomorrow afternoon. I presume visiting hours are still from 2 o'clock?"

"Yes, that's right. Thank you, Frank. I need to see you. Two o'clock tomorrow, then. I can't wait."

For the rest of the day, Erica relaxed, happy in the knowledge that her brother was soon to visit her.

The following day, she took extra care in her

appearance, wanting to make sure she looked her best so as to hopefully take away some of his worry about her. Her admiration for her older brother by five years had been in place since she was a young girl. Bryan had thought the world of him as well, and they'd spent many happy times together during their adult years. The fact that he also lived in Bournemouth had made it easy for their relationship to stay strong, especially after their parents' deaths.

She glanced at her watch. Twelve o'clock. Still two hours to wait.

Her mind drifted back to their childhood and the wonderful memories of the happy days spent with her mum, dad and Frank. How perfect and easy their lives had been.

She sat on a bench in the gardens and awaited Frank's arrival. It was eerily quiet out there … traffic, thankfully, a distant memory. A bird landed on the ground nearby. It had a black head, white cheeks, a green back and a black stripe down its front. She identified it immediately as a Great Tit. It began to sing, it's tail pumping up and down.

Frank strolled towards Erica and shouted, "Hey, sis. You're looking good."

There was a knot in her stomach as she reached up to hug her brother.

"It's so good to see you. I've been struggling to think straight for such a long time," she said.

"I have to admit, it's been an anxious time for everyone. It's gone on for far longer than the other episodes, and Dr. Horne told me it was the worst she'd ever seen you."

"I don't know how or why it happens," Erica said.

"I just want you home ... out of here. I want you to come and live with me until you're well enough to pick up the pieces on your own."

"Four months, that's all. Dr. Horne says if I can stay well, like I am, for four months, they'll consider discharging me."

A sick feeling in her stomach churned as she registered just how much she would love to be well enough to live with Frank.

"Have you called Laurence? He's been so worried about you?"

"I haven't spoken to him in such a long time. Do you think he'll mind if I give him a call?"

She tried to gather her thoughts.

"I just want to see you happy again, and so does Laurence."

"I'll never be the same *me* ... the same Erica. It's like I'm someone else ... somewhere else."

"Your heart's been broken losing Bryan. Of course, it's painful for you."

"It's not like it's even just broken. It's like it's been physically ripped out of me and shredded into a million pieces."

"I know. I understand. I thought the world of him. It's been a pretty significant loss in my life, too, but you still have Laurence and me who both love you."

"I know. I need to stop wallowing and being so full of self-pity. I also desperately need to stop inventing sub-versions of myself."

"Yes. It's become a pattern of behaviour that's extremely concerning."

"I'm just so scared of who my future self might be."

"Well, your memory seems fine at the moment. Just try and keep it that way."

"It's my brain using some type of defence mechanism, trying to block out my truth, I guess. Do you remember our trip to New York: the three of us, you, me and Bryan? How moved were we as we stood by the pools that mark the footprint of the Twin Towers, the names of the dead inscribed around the edge, and now, Bryan – that's all he is now – a memory inscribed on his headstone, one I've never even managed to visit. The High-Line!

A PARALLEL PERSONA

Do you remember what a lovely afternoon we had walking and eating ice creams along the disused railway tracks? The Empire State Building, Brooklyn Bridge, Central Park, and then the amazing helicopter ride over Manhattan, observing the steel and glass skyscrapers and the yellow taxis, which looked like Dinky toys swarming through the streets. Ellis Island, learning about the immigrants; the baseball game Bryan insisted on us watching. What a spectacle and atmosphere that was! We stayed in that unique, boutique hotel in the heart of Midtown Manhattan. These are the memories I want to keep. I don't want to lose my memories of the fun we had together."

"Do you recall his allotment … the one he liked to call his secret garden?"

"Yes," she smiled. "It was so precious to him. He was so passionate about our growing our own fruit and vegetables, strawberries, leeks, tomatoes, peppers, onions and lavender. He was going to take on another allotment, when I opened the flower restaurant, to supply most of the fresh ingredients we would need."

"He was a strong man, but he had a lovely soft side to his personality," Frank said.

"Nothing was ever too much trouble for him."

"Maybe, when you get discharged, we could look for an allotment for you? Maybe it's something you would enjoy doing in memory of Bryan?"

"Are you still working on your cars, Frank?"

"Yep. Still turning rust into riches, restoring luxury cars and selling them on."

"Frank, I need one of your bubble wrap hugs, please."

He leant over and hugged Erica tightly.

"My heart fills with bubbles every time I see you."

Erica's eyes lit up. It was a gesture and a saying they'd shared since she was a little girl.

"You need to be brave now, sis. Get better … get stronger. It's time to come home."

"I know. I can always count on you to be there for me. I'm going to call Laurence this evening … let him know I'm okay. I still dream of owning my own flower restaurant one day. I'm determined to stay well this time. I'm ready to come home."

"Remember how you used to love to help mum in the kitchen, when you were a little kid?" Frank asked.

"Yeah. I want to be able to start

experimenting with food again."

"Well, come on home soon and you can cook for me."

She smiled at him, his presence having made her feel cheerful, warm and calm. She really was grateful to have such a wonderful brother. If only she could continue to feel this way.

The bell rang to signal that visiting time was over.

"When will I see you next?" she asked.

Chapter 22

Despite wanting to speak with Laurence, Erica's finger hesitated over the screen of her phone. It felt like it had been such a long time. Would he still be friendly towards her? She'd always known she'd been lucky to have such a good friend in her life, ever since she'd first met him when she was nine years old. Feeling super self-conscious, her finger pressed 'dial'. The ringtone cut to voicemail, and she felt immediately deflated, hanging up without leaving a message. His northern accent and sense of humour rung in her ears. She missed him. What if he didn't want to be her friend any longer? Maybe he'd given up on her? She picked up her apron and headed towards her art therapy class, leaving her phone on the bedside cabinet to charge.

After acknowledging the art therapist, Denise, she moved towards an available easel and canvas, and began to put her own personal problems into her painting. She was soon lost in the therapeutic pleasure of applying paint to canvas. Denise never insisted on any careful planning of what she expected during therapy, but she encouraged them to use their imagination to paint or draw spontaneously whatever they desired. She told them to allow the brush to tell a story. They were to daydream and listen to what was inside them, and then just let it flow out onto the canvas. She advised them to feel their emotions, and find what was deep in their minds, even their faults, and then convey them onto the canvas along with their positive thoughts. They should let go of their insecurities and stress, let go of any past hurts, and celebrate any recent achievements or successes.

As she painted, she thought about the coping techniques and strategies her brain had used to avoid the trauma and painful, difficult emotions. It was obviously some type of defence mechanism, whereby she imagined living a totally different life. But how did her mind trick her into believing these stories? Was it by experiencing somebody else's imagined pain that she escaped from her own?

What would the reality of tomorrow be for her? Dare she even start facing her future, or would she imprison herself in another world of virtual reality? Would she be able to deny herself a parallel persona? If only she could reconnect with the real world and stay that way.

One thing she knew she really had to overcome was the poisonous effect of the guilt she felt around the accident.

Her raw emotion spilled out onto the canvas ... all of her flaws and imperfections. From now on, she would tell herself no more lies. She would live a life of honesty.

She sat upright and stared at her painting. She smiled. It was full of optimism and hope. From now on, she would give life her all. She was determined to see this situation out to its end, no matter how uncomfortable it made her feel. Yes, she was scared of her own future and reality, but she would not allow fear to rule her life any longer. Rain or shine, she would not let Frank down again. She would no longer reject herself and her future life. No more self-imposed suffering.

Erica's release into the painting had triggered an inner peace – a calmness and understanding of her situation. Her mind had finally relaxed.

Back in the solitude of her room, she stood under the hot water of her shower and contemplated her life and what it held for her. She didn't have any money worries, thanks to her inheritance, and her apartment had been managed by Frank during her stay in the hospital, so she had made a good income from it, because he had rented it out.

Frank! She was so lucky to have him. And Laurence! Hopefully, he'd still be a good friend to her. She would try and call him again later. And she was so grateful to Frank for his offer for her to live with him for a while … how lovely that would be.

She thought about all the positive things in her life. Her books and love of reading and cooking. Flowers and gardens, and her enjoyment of being outside in nature. The fact that she'd been terribly ill, mentally, but that Dr. Horne and Dr. Eliott had managed to keep her safe. The kindness of the nurses towards her, especially her favourite, Leta. The memories of the holidays with Bryan, nobody could steal those away from her. The hopes of still being able to one day open her flower restaurant. Her love of music and her ability to lose herself in its emotions. Her love of hiking and walking, taking in the beauty of her surroundings. Oh, and art therapy. Hadn't that just given her the breakthrough she needed on her path to recovery?

Time was running out. Why had she wasted so much of it? A mantra sprang into her mind.

"A journey of a thousand miles begins with a single step."

It was time to take that step … to remember who she was.

As she exited the shower, her phone rang. The screen showed that it was Laurence, but she pressed 'decline'. She would call him back shortly. Relief overcame her. It looked as though he hadn't given up on her as a friend.

She made herself a coffee and got dressed into her blue-and-white cotton kimono. Sitting on her bed, feet up, she dialled his number.

Erica sipped her coffee, the goodness of it hitting the back of her throat, making her feel happy for the first time in a long time. She heard the compassion in Laurence's voice immediately.

"Erica, is that you? Frank told me we've got you back. You don't know how relieved I am."

"I'm so sorry I've put you and Frank through all this again."

"I've missed you. I've missed your lovely smile," he said.

"Are you coming to visit? I promise I'm determined to stay well this time."

She took another gulp of her coffee.

A PARALLEL PERSONA

After concluding their conversation, she sat back on her bed and took in the surroundings of her room, thinking about Laurence and what an amazing friend he'd been to her by sticking by her and accepting the flaws that her character had developed since Bryan's death. Now it was time for her to accept her own flaws and deal with them. She couldn't put Frank or Laurence through this again, nor indeed herself. It was time to start appreciating life once more. Erica couldn't give up now, she needed to push herself through this and get well so that she could leave the hospital and go and live with Frank. She would not allow Bryan's death to harden her heart. It could no longer have this impact on her well-being. She would do it for Frank and Laurence, for the people she cared about.

Her eyes closed as she fell asleep, knowing in her heart that tomorrow was worth waking up for.

The following morning, she awoke having slept soundly without any need for medication. She was proud that she no longer needed to take anything during the daytime either. Sitting opposite Dr. Horne, she explained how she was feeling.

"It's time to face my truth … to start to understand who I really am without Bryan in my life. It's time for me to heal. I want to leave here as soon as possible to go and live with Frank."

"It's so good to see you so well and hear you being so positive. The healing has definitely started from within," Dr. Horne replied looking at her watch. "How would you feel about us trying to arrange a visit to Frank's for a couple of hours this week-end?"

Stunned into silence, unable to comprehend the words and articulate at the same time, Erica nodded her approval.

"I'll take that as a yes, then. I'll try and make the arrangements with Frank and let you know."

Dr. Horne stood up.

"You're doing really well. Now, I'm sorry to cut this short, but I've a managerial conference call to make."

Back in her room, Erica didn't dare to think that she could be leaving the hospital this weekend, even if only for a couple of hours. Had she imagined the words that had tumbled out of Dr. Horne's mouth? Had she heard properly?

Leta entered her room.

"Are you okay, Hun? Great news, I hear!

Being allowed out of here for a bit. It's so good to see you so well."

"I can't believe it, Leta. I thought I'd imagined Dr. Horne saying that I could go out."

"It'll do you good to get out of here for a bit. You've been here way too long."

"Yeah. My life has been like some sort of lame joke, hasn't it?"

"It'll be lovely for you to spend some time with your brother, away from this place. I've never thought of it as particularly healthy for anyone to have to stay here for so long."

All afternoon, Erica had to keep telling herself over and over that this was real. She was being allowed out.

Mina knocked on her door.

"Hi! Can I come in? I can't tell you how relieved I am to see you looking so well. The stress you've caused me, you wouldn't believe."

"I'm so sorry. Was I horrible to you?"

"Don't you remember any of it?"

"I'd rather not talk about it, if that's okay with you?"

Mina shot her a friendly smile.

"Of course. That's fine. All that matters now

is that you're well, and we need to make sure you stay that way."

"What's the film in the day room this evening? I thought I might like some company tonight."

Meeting this comment with enthusiasm, Mina's tongue ran away with the description of the film, adding, "I might even see if I can come and join you to watch it."

Keeping to her word, Mina slipped into the chair next to Erica's ten minutes into the film.

"I knew you'd get better eventually ... that your mind would come back to us," she whispered into Erica's left ear.

A garden of red roses filled the television screen. Erica leaned forward almost wanting to touch them. They reminded her of the flowers in her Mother's garden. The red roses were just the same. The film continued to consume her until she was lost in a wonderland of fiction.

Later, tucked into bed, the falling asleep part was easier said than done. She was too wired from the film, and from her excitement at the prospect of going to Frank's at the weekend. It was only Monday night, which meant at least four more nights after this one, depending on whether Frank agreed Saturday or Sunday with Dr. Horne.

A PARALLEL PERSONA

She checked her watch. It was one o'clock in the morning and she was still lying there, her mind racing about how it would feel to leave the hospital, even if just for a couple of hours. She woke the next morning feeling exhausted; she'd barely slept at all.

By Wednesday, her excitement had increased even further when Dr. Horne informed her that Frank would be collecting her at 2pm on Saturday, and they had agreed that, as long as everything went well, he wouldn't return her until 6pm. A whole four hours of freedom lay before her.

She did a full exercise workout to try and burn off some of the excess energy she was feeling. Having not slept well for the previous two nights, she almost literally passed out as soon as her head touched the pillow. *'Only two more nights to go after this one'* was her final thought as she descended into a heavy sleep.

On Thursday, she woke up feeling much better from a good night's rest. Friday arrived, and the glimmer of it really happening intensified. She could even smell it in her nostrils. She confined herself to her bedroom for the day and evening. She couldn't afford for one of the other patients to interfere and make her react to something that might prevent her visit from taking place.

Her mood and energy levels were playing havoc with her mind. She exercised some more, attempting to make the time move quickly. She ate dinner off a tray in her room and watched TV on her own.

Saturday arrived! Happy Frank day! The day was finally here!

The morning passed surprisingly fast as she busied herself with a full pamper session, making herself look the best she could to spend some time with her brother.

"It's a beautiful day," Frank said, as Erica jumped into the passenger seat of his car. "We've four hours. I thought you might like to hike instead of just sitting around. You've done so much of that over the past years."

"I'd love that more than anything, but I don't own any hiking boots anymore."

"Yes, you do. Look on the back seat. I bought you a new pair … and some socks."

"You're too good to me. Thank you so much. It will be so lovely hiking again. I've missed it so much."

She leant into the back of the car, retrieved the socks and boots and placed them on her feet.

"You even remembered my shoe size," she

said.

After a 20-minute drive, they reached a pub car park. Frank pulled in and parked the car. They followed a footpath bearing left through a bridle gate into a field, and then they walked straight ahead through a small poplar wood before they came across a pond. Frank removed his backpack.

"I thought we could sit here for a while. I brought sandwiches and drinks for us."

Erica sat and breathed in the rich, earthy smell of the countryside. Her voice wanted to cry out in exaltation. She stretched out her hand to feel the grass beneath her. Her face was glowing like a burning spear. If only she could capture the moment forever. This was now her future. A sea of tranquillity washed over her.

Frank handed her a sandwich.

"Speak to me … open up … tell me your thoughts," he said.

"Do you think I've gone completely crazy?" she asked.

"Why would you think that? You're totally rational at the moment, but you've been extremely ill and had some type of psychological reaction to Bryan's death. I've never once thought you were crazy."

"So let's not let it all be about me. How's life been treating you?" she asked.

"Not much has changed, to be honest. I just want you, and need you, back in it full-time."

"No lady on the horizon then?"

"I've recently broken up with one. You know it's always been the same; they never turn out to be the right one. Guess I've always been rubbish at choosing one I could really fall in love with. Mum and Dad, you and Bryan … I think you all set my standard too high," he smiled.

"I'm going to stay strong this time … take one day at a time and keep moving forward," she said.

"Well, the next step is to get you home, to come and live with me."

"I'm improving so much this time. I spoke with Laurence on the phone. He was going away on a business trip, but as soon as he's back, he'll be coming to see me."

"I can see that you are making rapid progress towards recovery."

"I need to understand that life can take unexpected turns, that you never know what to expect. But the fear of what could happen shouldn't prevent me from actually living my life."

"I'm just so happy to be able to spend these few hours with you, away from that dreaded hospital," Frank said.

"Yeah! The memories aren't great, are they?"

She could feel the tears forming, her hands beginning to shake and a chill running down her spine as her voice wavered.

"After all that's happened, none of this is easy for either of us," he said, his tone weary and pessimistic.

Chapter 23

Today was the first time she'd seen Laurence since her ongoing recovery. She was excited beyond belief that once again she was being allowed to leave the hospital, only this time in the trusted care of her friend.

She'd taken extra care with her hair and make-up. She wanted to look her best, and having gained a few pounds, she was relatively happy with her appearance. He'd suggested a pub lunch and she'd readily agreed, thrilled at the prospect of his company and a meal outside of the hospital.

On the journey to the pub, there had been a lot of small talk between them, but now that they were sitting opposite one another and had ordered their food, they began to properly open up.

Sipping her orange juice, she filled him in on her news and then said, "So, now you know all about me, but you've not told me much about what's been happening in your life whilst I've been ill."

"Well, my business life and my home are still as you will remember, but there is an addition to my life that you probably won't recall."

Erica didn't know why, but her heart sank. An addition? Did he mean he'd got married or something? If he had, shouldn't she be feeling pleased for him?

"I have a child, Erica. A little boy … Benjamin. He's almost three."

"Wow! That's amazing! And your wife's name? I presume you married?"

"Unfortunately, the relationship didn't work out, but I have Benjamin every other weekend."

"Oh! I'm so sorry."

Erica didn't understand why she felt a sense of relief.

"It's okay. The relationship has gone, but I have a beautiful son, and I can't wait for you to meet him. He's an absolute treasure."

The couple of hours they had together passed quickly, and all too soon for Erica, she found herself deposited safely back at the hospital and in the solitude of her own room. Laurence had bought her some flowers, and she took great pleasure in arranging them in her vase, only to rearrange them once more as she contemplated the news of Laurence being a father.

Erica's freedom within the hospital grounds had increased, her movements no longer monitored or supervised. Discussions had begun about her discharge. She was to live with Frank as an interim arrangement.

She enjoyed exploring the gardens, especially the ones which had been restricted to her beforehand. She had found a secret garden at the very back of the hospital, where she spent most of her time. It was so peaceful there, and nobody else ever seemed to visit this little haven that she'd carved out for herself. In this space, surrounded by plants, trees and flowers, she used her time to reflect on her loss of Bryan and what little she could remember about the accident. She was slowly coming to terms with facing her true reality and the weird way that her mind had reacted to the trauma. She began to realise that her mental state had caused the loss of her freedom and her own personal privileges. It was time for her to fight for her natural human rights to be restored; her sanity had returned.

Later the same day, she sat with Dr. Horne and discussed these rights further. Although, in principle, Dr. Horne agreed with Erica, she testily reminded her of just how mentally ill she had been and how the doctors were still fearful of rushing things and causing any type of relapse.

"So," Erica asked, "can I have an actual date for leaving here and moving in with Frank? I'm absolutely ready. I believe now it's doing me more harm than good by staying here."

"Well, we certainly wouldn't want you to suffer any more agony by staying here unnecessarily. I'm sure the panel will approve your discharge. It's on the agenda for tomorrow's meeting. With Frank's written care plan in place, I can't see why your fairly immediate discharge wouldn't be approved," Dr. Horne said. "Try and get a good night's sleep, and I will come and inform you of the panel's decision straight after the meeting tomorrow."

Back in her room, Erica decided it was time to start sorting out her belongings. Most of them she associated with the hospital and didn't want to take with her when she left. It would feel good to donate most of her things to the other patients. She decided to buy everything new when she moved in with Frank. It would be a fresh start.

Erica drew her curtains and climbed into bed.

Tomorrow couldn't come quick enough for her.

Her thoughts drifted to Frank and Laurence. She was so thankful that neither of them had deserted her, and that both were still committed to being a part of her life. If the meeting the following day went in her favour, she could be out of the hospital and living with Frank in less than a week. Her mind ran wild with this thought and for a few hours any chance of sleep evaded her.

Easter was fast approaching, and having finally drifted off, her dream involved spending it with Frank, Laurence and sharing chocolate eggs with the little boy, Benjamin, whom she had yet to meet.

The following morning, as she headed to the canteen to collect her breakfast, she overheard Leta and Mina gossiping. She moved in closer to them but managed to stay out of sight. They were discussing her, and she was relieved to hear them both agree that the panel should allow her discharge ... that she had been there long enough, and she was definitely well enough to leave.

As she ate her breakfast, she considered the possibility that the panel could make the wrong decision and her discharge would be refused. She wasn't sure how she would handle such a situation. It would surely destroy her. Her thoughts began to drift back to the darkest of days, when her illness had been at its worst. She couldn't go back to that place ever again. Her mental state now depended on her discharge. But could she trust Dr. Horne and Dr. Eliott to persuade the panel that she was fit for it?

Lunchtime arrived and there had still been no word from Dr. Horne. Erica had paced her room back and forth … back and forth. Every time she looked at her watch, the fingers didn't appear to have moved.

Beside herself with anguish, she went in search of Leta. Locating her in the laundry room, she burst out, "Have you heard anything? Are they still in the meeting?"

"Calm down, Erica. Are you aware this is the fifth time you've asked me this morning? As I've told you every time, Dr. Horne will come and see you immediately after it finishes. Yours isn't the only case they have to consider. There will be an agenda with other items to be discussed."

Erica began to shake, and as she went to take a step away from Leta, it almost sent her sprawling. Leta caught her arm quickly.

"C'mon, Erica. Let's steady you up. You're getting yourself into a state."

"I'm unsure about what I'm meant to be doing whilst I wait. It's driving me crazy … not knowing."

Her gaze settled on Leta.

"I know, but for the time being, you need to try and relax."

Chapter 24

Erica turned on the television in her room to try and distract herself from the fact that it was now *way* after lunchtime, but she still hadn't heard anything from Dr. Horne. Finding no solace on the TV screen, she switched it off, picked up a book, turned to the first page and started to read. Ninety-five percent of the first chapter didn't sink in. It was no good; her mind wouldn't budge from her fixation on what the panel's decision would be.

She was ready to leave this place and become a new person. Surely they could see that. She was ready to welcome happiness back into her life again … with her family, good health and a new lifestyle.

Didn't they know what was good for her? Why couldn't they come to a decision? What on earth could they still be discussing? Her life had fallen apart, but she intended to get it all back on track. She was stable, and she would feel even more stable once she was settled in at Frank's home.

She could wait no longer. She would have to go and find Dr. Horne. The wait was killing her. This was her life, and from this day forward, she intended to live it.

Just as she was plucking up the courage to go and find Dr. Horne, she appeared in Erica's doorway.

"I'm so sorry it took so long," she said. "There was an awful lot of business on today's agenda. I also took the liberty of speaking with Frank to confirm a few details before I spoke with you.

"Anyway, it's great news. You'll be moving out of here tomorrow. Frank insisted that, as the discharge has been granted, it should be at the earliest possible opportunity.

"I imagine that you will greet this news with a certain degree of jubilation, but I would ask that you do not upset the other patients and stir-up any feelings of jealousy at your home-going."

"Well, hells-bells! I can't believe it! Tomorrow, you say? That's earlier than I'd even dared to dream of.

"Thank you, Dr. Horne! And thank you for

all you have done for me whilst I was ill."

The following day, installed in Frank's home, Erica kept peering at Frank, whilst he was busying himself sorting everything out to make her stay as comfortable as possible. She still couldn't believe it was true. She was in Frank's home, and no longer an inpatient at the hospital.

"I'll need to go shopping. I've left most of my stuff at the hospital. I wanted it to be a fresh start. A whole new wardrobe … a whole new me!

"I'm so happy to be here. Thanks so much. Shall I start preparing dinner? I want to be as helpful as I can whilst I'm living here."

"There's plenty of time for all that. I've got a bottle of Dom Perignon that I've been keeping on ice for this very occasion. Let's crack that open and just enjoy each other's company."

Frank poured them both a glass and sat down next to her on the sofa. They clinked glasses and toasted the fact that she was out of hospital.

"So tell me more about Laurence. I was so shocked when he told me he had a little boy … Benjamin. How's he coping with that? And what's she like? The mother."

"A right bitch, to be honest. Treated

Laurence like shit. He proposed to her, you know, when she told him she was pregnant. She turned him down, though. In my opinion, she just uses him as a babysitter, so that she can go out and get pissed. She drains him of money, too. Benjamin's gorgeous though. Such a little character."

"What's her name? The mother! I don't like the sound of her. I hope our paths don't cross. I'm not sure I'd be able to hold my tongue, treating our Laurence like that."

"Her name's Carolina! I'd stay well clear of her. As I say, she's a nasty piece of work."

"Does she live nearby?"

"No. That's another thing. She's 70 miles away, but she expects Laurence to do all the travelling. Says if he wants to see Benjamin, it's up to him to collect and return him."

The doorbell rang. Frank looked at his watch.

"Oh shit! With all the excitement of picking you up, I forgot that I had a car being dropped off today."

"No worries! You go and deal with it, and I'll see what I can find to cook us for dinner."

Once in the kitchen and having had a good rummage in the cupboards to get her bearings and to discover what food was available for dinner, a sense of total peace and happiness embraced Erica. Why had she struggled so much with Bryan's death? Why had she put herself and Frank through all this turmoil? She intended to make up for it to both Frank and Laurence. She would insist on doing all the chores for Frank and make him some mouth-watering dinners. She'd make sure that he didn't regret having her to live with him. And as for Laurence, well, she'd try and return some of the support he'd given her.

Her phone buzzed, Laurence's name flashed across the screen.

"Hi," she answered.

"Hi. Great news! You're home! I'd like to take you out to celebrate one night this week. I thought we could go to the cinema and then for a meal."

"Oh, absolutely! That would be great. Shall we say Thursday? That would give me a chance to settle down here for a couple of days."

"Yeah, great. I'll pick you up at 7 on Thursday then. That okay?"

"Yeah, sure. Look forward to seeing you."

In the kitchen, her abilities were speedily recovered and the dinner she was putting together was coming along well.

Frank entered the room.

"Wow! Smells good! I see you've not lost your touch. I don't need to direct you to where anything is then, by the looks of it."

"Just get out my kitchen and leave me to it," Erica laughed.

"And how many times have I heard you say that, sis?" Frank smiled.

"Yeah! And you know the consequences of not doing as you're told," she laughed, chasing him out of the doorway.

Erica returned to mixing her batter, a broad smile spreading across her face as the frying pan heated up.

After dinner, they both collapsed onto the sofa to watch a movie. During an x-rated scene, which was supposed to be romantic, their common sense of humour surfaced as they fell about laughing together at the woman in suspenders, lying on the kitchen table holding a rolling-pin in her hand.

In a voice saturated with laughter, Erica said, "I'm okay, aren't I? I'm going to be okay."

Chapter 25

A knock at Frank's door signalled that Laurence had arrived to take her out to the cinema and then for a meal.

After finding a parking space, which was next to impossible in the underground car park, they headed up the escalator to the second floor of the shopping mall, where the cinema was located. They took their place in the queue to purchase the tickets.

Erica caught sight of herself in a glass window. It was a strange feeling to be around so many people, but she could do this ... of course, she could ... especially with Laurence at her side.

Only ten minutes into the film, a horror that they'd both wanted to see, Erica squealed at a moment of suspense, and Laurence chuckled at her response.

She gave him a disapproving look that quickly melted into a smile.

Her mind wandered. What would it be like to run her hands over Laurence's body the way she had Bryan's? ... to feel him like a lover.

Checking herself, she thought that maybe one day she'd find somebody like Bryan. But it couldn't be Laurence. He was her friend and had been Bryan's close mate as well.

Registering her thoughts, it dawned on her that she was no longer an empty vessel, craving Bryan to be alive once more. She was beginning to recognise that it was time to let him go and focus on her own future ... a future with him no longer by her side to hold her hand.

Her attention returned to the film, and she observed the handprints on the windows, as if someone had tried to escape, and blood spattered on the ceilings and walls. Maybe the choice of a horror film had not been such a clever one; she was almost shaking with fear as to what was going to happen next. It would be a challenge to sit through the rest of the film without squealing out loud, or worse still, embarrassing herself by running out of the cinema altogether.

Shifting uncomfortably in her chair, she

moved a little closer to Laurence.

Back at the car, Laurence paused at the driver's door, key in hand.

"Are you sure you're okay? Are you still happy to go to a restaurant as well?"

"Yes," she replied, her gaze going from him to the passenger door.

Fear clutched at her heart with cold fingers. She could do this. It was just dinner with her good friend, Laurence.

She hurriedly climbed into the passenger seat.

Why did she feel so uneasy? This was crazy. She had to get herself back under control.

"I don't know what's bothering you, Erica, but if I've done something wrong or said something to upset you, I wish you would tell me."

Looking at him as if he'd betrayed her, she said, "I'm sorry, Laurence. Maybe I'm just not ready for all this just yet."

"Let's get you home to Frank, then," he said.

As they drove back in silence, an ambulance wailed past them, and images of their car accident flooded into Erica's mind.

Moving forward in life without him was clearly still going to be more of a struggle than she'd previously envisaged.

As the journey continued, she became more and more distant, her heart beating fast. Annoyed with herself, she felt like a child … out of her depth in a grown-up's world.

Closing her eyes, she hoped that her behaviour wouldn't impact too much on her relationship with Laurence.

Chapter 26

The following morning, Erica put on a pair of jeans and a T-shirt.

The new circumstances she found herself living in, with Frank and away from the hospital, gave her a happy glow and the consequences of such felt like a great victory in itself.

Skipping down the stairs, she greeted Frank in the kitchen, washing out the coffee pot.

"Morning. Are you hungry? I'll get us some breakfast."

"No thanks, sis. I've got work to do today. I try not to eat too much at breakfast time. Got to keep the weight down, you know." He patted his stomach. "Just sort yourself out."

"Okay! I thought I might head into town on my own, today. I need to learn to manage to do things on my own. I can't rely on you every day."

Although the kitchen was clean and airy, Erica decided to give it a good spring-clean after she'd eaten her breakfast.

"I'm off then," Frank called as he peered into the kitchen.

"Oh my," he laughed. "Your OCD is kicking in nicely, then?"

She threw the cloth she was using straight at him.

"Don't laugh at me! I know it's clean! But you know how I like things to be spotless."

"Well, as long as you're happy! It's good to have you around. I'll catch you later. I'll be back about five."

As soon as he left, she headed upstairs to make herself look decent for her trip into town.

Feeling fairly relaxed, she decided she would walk the 30-minute route into the centre.

Closing the front door behind her, she attempted to move her feet as she turned her body for a clearer view down the street. But they wouldn't move, it was as though they were fixed to the drive.

Anxiety closed in on her rapidly. She wasn't ready to do this … not on her own. What had she been thinking? She quickly put the key into the lock of the front door and turned it, gasping with relief as she stepped back inside the hallway.

Once more, fear had clutched at her heart with its ice-cold fingers. How was she ever going to overcome this?

Back in the safety of Frank's home, she felt comfortable again, and she knew that, once he was home, she would feel even better.

Erica put on some music to ease the silence.

All the best of her had belonged to Bryan. Somehow she had to find a way through life without him.

It was a disturbing thought. She realised she hadn't truly grieved. All she'd done was to have some type of psychotic episode, inventing a persona that didn't really exist. Now it was time for her to face the reality of the situation as Erica.

Determination was now her mantra. She mustn't allow herself to go down the slippery slope and end up back in hospital. She took a deep breath. She'd come this far, and she must keep moving forwards.

She set a glass of coke on the kitchen counter before her and sat on the bar stool watching the bubbles rising to the top.

A knock at the front door broke her thoughts. Laurence's familiar face was a pleasant surprise.

"Thought I'd check-in on you, seeing as you weren't too great last night."

"C'mon in. I'm sorry about last night. I was doing my best not to let things get out of control. I'm in a better place than I was, but I'm still really struggling."

She studied his face, trying to read his reaction.

"We can talk about it if it helps. You can tell me why you needed to carve out a false identity for yourself."

Chapter 27

Erica began to cry.

Laurence took her arms and guided her to a chair in the lounge, where he handed her a fistful of tissues and knelt down beside her.

"C'mon. It's good to have someone to talk to. Just let it all out," Laurence said.

He touched her hand and a familiar warmth floated through her, easing the pain.

"It's difficult for me to share my feelings … to talk about the past. It's as though I'm living a daily nightmare."

Laurence leant up and kissed her on the cheek.

"I care about you. In fact, I've never stopped caring about you all the time you've been ill."

"I'm going through so many changes. I tried to go into town on my own, and I couldn't even do that."

She raised her shaking fingers to her mouth.

"Just look at that beautiful blue sky up there. Let me take you into town. Let's not waste the day. It's not what Bryan would have wanted for you."

He smiled, gripping her elbow with his warm hand.

"Okay," she said, trying to smile back.

"Give me a few minutes to dry my eyes and re-apply a bit of make-up."

"Good,' he said cheerfully. "I'll wait right here for you."

She steadied herself as she stood up, feeling a little dizzy.

As they walked into town, Laurence said, "By the way, it's going to be Benjamin's third birthday soon. I'd like you to meet him and also to help plan a little party for him, if you're up to it?"

"Oh, I'd love that, Laurence. Thank you for asking me. I'll make him a cake. We can get some decorations and balloons. How many guests will there be? We could organise a few games."

Her legs were trembling as she walked, but

she was determined to keep going. She wasn't going to let Laurence down again, not when he kept showing her such consideration and kindness.

The first shop Erica wanted to go into was a bookshop.

With Laurence at her side, she began to relax. She no longer felt so vulnerable. She was determined to succeed, not only through persistence, but also by accepting the support that Frank and Laurence were offering her.

An assistant approached them.

"Can I help you? Were you looking for a particular type of book?" she asked.

"Yes," Erica replied. "A birthday cake recipe book, but one which specialises in children's cakes."

At the thought of baking Benjamin a birthday cake, a warmth began to flow through her veins and her heart pounded with more excitement than it had for a very long time.

Finally, she felt herself to be of use to someone. She was doing something positive.

Chapter 28

Erica was in desperate need of new underwear, but she questioned herself as to whether it would be too personal to shop for it with Laurence in tow.

Cake book in hand, she decided it would be best left for another day, and not particularly wanting to go inside any more shops, she suggested they go for a walk.

Laurence's bright smile at her suggestion indicated that she had made the right choice. He probably couldn't think of anything worse than being dragged around shops with her.

"It's nice to have someone to walk with. Since I split up with Carolina, life's been a bit lonely for me," he said.

"I'm sorry. I've been so selfish … so wrapped up in my own problems. I hadn't given much thought to what you've gone through. It can't have been easy splitting-up … and with a child to consider as well."

"Yes, she soon tossed me to one side. I couldn't see her for who she really was. I was too besotted with her looks to see what lay beneath the surface."

Glancing over at him as they walked, she noted that he was dressed all in black, a colour that should have minimized his size, but instead it served to amplify how muscular he was beneath the clothing.

Their walk took them past a mosque, a church, the weekly market, and then further out of town towards the woods.

Glancing down at her sandaled feet, it occurred to her that she was hardly dressed appropriately. Despite this she felt happy inside. She was enjoying his company.

They entered a clearing with a pond and found a pathway that would take them deeper into the woods. It was pleasant not to have anything particular to do … to just be able to amble along as if she hadn't care in the world. Nature had always managed to make her feel better, and she felt safe with Laurence walking beside her.

"This is wonderful. It's so nice to be able to enjoy being outside like this. I've missed this so much," Erica said.

It felt good to have her emotions under control.

"I don't know what I saw in her, you know. But at least one good thing came out of it, and that's Benjamin."

"Well, she's a fool! She should have been happy to be with a man with the qualities you have. Would you like to come over tomorrow night and have dinner with Frank and me? I'll cook something special for us all, just like I used to."

"Definitely, I'd love to. I've missed the deliciousness of your cooking. There's nobody who can cook the way you do.

"Talking of which are you getting hungry? Should we head back and find somewhere in town for a late lunch?"

He bent his head and his lips questioned hers … gently at first, and then with more passion as she responded.

His embrace was both warm and exciting, and yet somehow she felt caught in a situation.

What had just happened was beyond her belief, and yet she knew it was real.

Chapter 29

How long could she go on pretending she didn't have feelings for Laurence?

With the exception of an occasional remark or glance, they walked back towards town.

Laurence suggested that they head for a little French bistro situated down one of the small side streets.

"Oh! That would be lovely," Erica said. "I'd forgotten about that place. Mom and I used to meet there for lunch years ago. Is it still open?"

"I'm so happy to be in your company and to see you so well," Laurence said.

"I'm so hungry. C'mon. Let's hurry up and get there," she said.

As she sat opposite him at a little corner table, there was no mistaking the devotion in his beautiful blue eyes.

Enthusiastically, she scrutinised the menu, which the waiter had handed to her.

Laurence smirked across the table at her.

"Great menu, isn't it? I knew you'd like it here."

He blew her a kiss over the top of the menu.

"It is, but it's not as good as the one I'm going to have. I still want to open my flower restaurant. I'm thinking that, if I manage to stay well for a couple of months, I'd like to think about getting my apartment back and then start looking for suitable premises for my project."

Erica looked up to find Laurence staring at her.

"Do you think that's wise, so soon?" he asked.

"I don't intend to waste any more of my life. I love that apartment, although it will be difficult to face the memories of Bryan. It's something I need to do, and the flower restaurant has always been my dream. I was so close to achieving it before."

"I'm thrilled you feel that way … that you're ready to live your own life again. I guess I'm just a little worried that you might be pushing yourself a bit too quickly, that's all," Laurence said.

"Thank you. Now let me look at the menu again. I'm going to have to stop myself from being too greedy and ordering more than I can eat."

Erica enjoyed her lunch and also Laurence's company. Both his sense and wit shone through his conversation. But as they walked back towards Frank's house, she surprised herself as the words tumbled out of her mouth.

"Laurence, I don't want to hurt you, and I don't want to get hurt either. But I think it's better for both of us if we just remain friends. I don't think I'm ready for anything more at the moment. I'm sorry."

"I can't help my feelings for you, Erica, but I completely understand."

Her voice cracked with the strain.

"You have made your feelings clear, but I'm just not in a position to go along with them."

"How do I earn your trust?" he asked.

"I admire your spirit and your passion, and it isn't that I don't trust you; it's more that I can't trust myself."

As they reached the front door to Frank's house, Laurence asked, "Can I at least give you a hug before you go inside?"

"Of course, and I'd still like you to come to

dinner tomorrow night, if that's okay with you."

"Thank you. I'd still like to ... as a friend."

She relaxed and hugged him back, and then watched as he climbed into his car and drove away.

Chapter 30

When Frank returned from work, Erica made them both a sandwich, explaining that she'd eaten a late lunch with Laurence.

"I'm going to make up for it tomorrow, though. I've invited him over to have dinner with us."

As Frank started to query her relationship with Laurence, she quickly cut him off.

"I'm sorry. I'm so tired. Do you mind if I go to my room? I need an early night."

"I've told you before, this is your home now. You can do as you please. You don't need my permission if you want to go to your room," Frank replied.

Erica lounged on her bed and read through the recipes in the cake book she'd bought earlier. It wasn't long before her eyes closed, and she dozed off to sleep.

The following morning, she dressed and arrived in the kitchen to find Frank already sitting at the breakfast bar, sipping a coffee.

He shook his head.

"Blimey! You must have really needed an early night. Did you sleep well?"

"I did, thanks. I thought I might do a fish dish for tonight. What do you think?"

"I always have an appetite for anything you cook, Erica," he said, lifting his chin to the glowing eyes across the kitchen.

She moved a few things off the breakfast bar to clear a space next to him.

"Oh! Forgive me," he said laughing. "Have I used a wrong towel or left too many dishes out?"

Laughing, she replied, "Laurence has asked me to make a cake for Benjamin's birthday. I can scarcely wait to get started on it."

She opened the cake book, which she'd brought downstairs with her, and showed Frank the one she'd selected.

"Look! This one's amazing."

"Oh! That's wonderful. Benjamin will love that."

Instantly, the familiar playful mood was back

between them.

"I can see I'm going to be obese by the time you move out of here," he joked.

"And in my opinion, you are well and truly on your way," she bantered back.

"I love you very much you know, Erica. It's such a relief to have you home."

Frank placed his mug in the sink.

"Right! I'm off. Don't get causing too much mayhem in the kitchen with your baking and cooking whilst I'm gone," he laughed.

Making herself at home, she soon felt free from any of her worries. She started with the cake, her plan being to head to the fishmongers in town at lunchtime, and then to prepare dinner in the afternoon. Lost in the baking, and with her face expressing her enjoyment, it reinforced her passion to go ahead with the restaurant. She was sure that her dream was the right thing to do.

Her excitement grew at the extravagance of the cake she'd decided to make. The morning passed quickly and before she knew it, she was in the fishmongers, selecting the fish for dinner. She was pleased that she'd made it this far on her own. The walk had been pleasant, and she'd experienced no anxieties.

The fishmonger turned to her.

"Oh, Erica! It's so lovely to see you. It's been so long. I heard you weren't well after Bryan's death. I'm so sorry."

Erica studied his lips as his apology tumbled out.

"Well, I couldn't have asked for a more pleasant greeting."

She smiled back at him.

"Thank you."

She felt the rise and fall of each breath, but she kept smiling. She had to keep this under control.

She paused only long enough to calm herself, and then pointed straight at the fish she required for their dinner.

Chapter 31

Erica studied the recipe for the dinner she was planning to serve.

She'd received a text message from Laurence confirming that he would be there around 6.

The afternoon flew by, and once she had everything under control, she headed upstairs to take a shower and change into something more suitable.

Pleased with her appearance, she headed back down and began to lay the dining room table for the three of them.

The room was hot and stuffy so she opened a couple of windows to ventilate it.

She wanted the table to look its best, so she took her time with the detail, her abundant imagination taking centre stage.

Standing back, she admired how lovely it looked, which once more reinforced her concept of how beautiful her restaurant would be. She felt certain of it. An urge to move on with her life overcame her.

Putting the finishing touches to the dinner, she hoped that Frank and Laurence would both have good appetites for the three courses she planned on serving them.

Frank returned home from work and remarked on how good she looked and how lovely it was to walk into the smell of a lovely dinner. He raced upstairs to shower and change his clothes.

Aglow with excitement at the sound of the doorbell, she rushed to the front door to greet Laurence.

As he entered the hallway, he handed her a bunch of flowers. He really did bring sunshine into her life. He always had, even when she'd been married to Bryan.

"I can't hide my feelings for you, Erica, so I'm not even going to attempt to," he said.

"Well, you're my most perfect friend in the entire world," she said, taking the flowers from him.

"How beautiful they are. Take a seat in the lounge whilst I go and find a vase. Frank will be down shortly. He's just gone to change."

Erica arranged the flowers in a vase and placed them on the dining room table, rearranging her centrepiece, as these did a much better job.

Again she stood back and admired her handiwork. The table was a delight to behold.

Returning to her guest in the lounge, she poured them both a glass of red wine, and they exchanged pleasantries, although Laurence was blatantly flirtatious as they waited for Frank to come downstairs and join them.

Chapter 32

"That dress really suits you," Laurence said.

Erica looked up at him.

"Thank you! I'll pop some music on."

Her search for the playlist she'd compiled earlier didn't take long, and soon afterwards peaceful background music began to play.

"I'm not harbouring any bad feelings towards you, Erica. If you're not ready for a relationship, I really do understand. I still love being in your company though."

His eyes dazzled her.

"What date in July did you say Benjamin's party is to be? I want to make sure I've got everything organised by then."

Frank entered the room.

"Hey, Laurence! Good to see you. Be lovely to have a good talk … the three of us, tonight."

A PARALLEL PERSONA

Erica paused before she poured Frank a glass of red wine, but as she did so, she smiled at him, noting how at ease he was with himself.

"We all deserve to be happy, and I believe the three of us are all very good at making each other feel that way," Laurence said.

Tiny flecks of dust danced across Erica's vision as the sunlight glared through the lounge window.

"I am truly blessed to have two such lovely men in my life."

She turned and left the room.

"I'll shout you when dinner's ready."

Feeling happy, she carried the starters through to the dining room and placed them on the table, realising how lucky she was to have Frank and Laurence's unconditional love and support. She was definitely feeling better now that life had turned a corner.

"Dinner's ready!" she called.

"Wow! The table looks so pretty," Laurence said as he took his seat.

Fiddling with her necklace, Erica took her seat and said, "Thank you."

"She always was the artistic one in the family," Frank jibed.

"I can't believe Benjamin's going to turn three next month. I think you should meet him before the party, Erica. Maybe we could plan a day together beforehand to give him chance to get to know you?" Laurence asked.

Erica dabbed at her brow with her serviette, the humidity and the heat of the day still feeling oppressive, even with the ventilation of the open windows.

"I'd love to. I truly want to get to know him and to help out with the party. I've already made a good start on his birthday cake."

"Great! I'll organise something then. I can't wait for you to meet him."

She relaxed and started to enjoy the evening feeling more normal, and less afraid, than she had in a long while. She ran a hand through her hair and smiled at Laurence.

"Could do with this weather turning a little cooler," Frank said.

And so the evening passed with old-world charm, tales of their past and present lives, and much laughter.

Slipping into her shoes, the day had come for Erica to meet Benjamin.

Laurence hadn't been around much in the

past couple of weeks, and Erica was excited to see him, realising how much she'd missed him.

With a sharp ear, she listened out for Laurence's car to pull onto the driveway. She felt emotional at the thought of meeting his son.

Five minutes later, she was greeting the tenderness of Benjamin's face, which closely resembled his father's.

Her heart raced as she glanced over at Laurence.

This boy with his golden hair melted her heart immediately as he hopped from one foot to the other with extraordinary energy.

"Hello, Erica. I'm Benjamin," he said, handing her a bunch of flowers.

"These are for you! I'm a fox. Do you want to hear me snarl?" he asked.

"I think I can be a fox as well," Erica said.

They snarled playfully at each other, and the rest of the day was spent exploring new haunts, exchanging secrets, making up games and building a tree house in Frank's garden.

Laurence smiled at her.

"He likes you. You're a natural with him."

Erica tilted the pretend crown on her head.

"Well, of course he does, don't you, Benjamin. After all, I am a princess."

Chapter 33

Erica woke at 2:00am, excited and nervous about Benjamin's party day ahead. It was to be held at Frank's house and whilst there were only a few guests, she was fully aware that Laurence's ex, Carolina, was to be present. Entertaining was Erica's forte, but when she'd volunteered to host the party, she hadn't for one minute realised that Laurence would invite Carolina.

After a restless night's sleep and a busy morning making final preparations, Erica slipped into the new dress she'd treated herself to for the occasion.

As she went downstairs, Laurence greeted her by taking her hand and kissing her palm.

"Thank you for doing all this for Benjamin and me. I really do appreciate it."

She smiled and rubbed her shoulder, which

felt tense from her lack of sleep and her eagerness to make sure nothing went wrong for Benjamin on his special day. Benjamin's birthday cake was on the table in the dining room, and Erica led Laurence and Benjamin through to show them her masterpiece.

The doorbell disturbed them; the guests were beginning to arrive.

Over-excited, Benjamin ran past them to the front door.

With a welcoming smile across her face, Erica greeted the first guests, who Laurence introduced as Lexi, Paul and their daughter, Esmee.

Esmee's exploring hands reached out for Benjamin's, and they ran off, hand in hand, to play together.

Frank appeared, clutching a bottle of Burgundy.

"Anyone for red?" he asked.

More guests arrived, with more children. The noise levels were becoming quite high, but Erica was mindful that there was still one very important guest yet to arrive … Carolina.

Benjamin excitedly began to open his presents.

"Shouldn't we wait for Carolina first?" Erica

asked Laurence.

As if awakening from a dream, he lifted his head and looked at her.

"Wait for Carolina! No, why would we? She knew the time she was supposed to be here. Her temperament is one of extremes; she blows hot and cold like the wind. If she turns up, she does. If she doesn't, then that's even better."

"I'll put the food out then, shall I?"

"Food's ready!" Erica shouted, as she placed chicken fingers, burgers, fries and her speciality apple pies on the table.

"Dive in, everyone. Help yourselves."

Her bright features were alert as she focused on the kids' faces, which were delighted by what she'd served them.

Frank took a burger from the table.

"This is great, sis. And the cake looks amazing!"

Erica sipped at her wine, trying to shove the notion of Carolina actually turning up now into the deepest recesses of her mind.

Putting his arm around her waist, Frank said, "I love you so much, Erica."

After most of the food had been devoured,

she heard the doorbell ring.

Carolina had finally arrived!

Busying herself with clearing away the table, Erica decided to leave it to Frank or Laurence to open the door and greet her ... although she couldn't help herself from eyeing her lean frame as she entered the hallway.

Chapter 34

Laurence introduced Carolina to Erica.

"I sincerely apologise for being so late," she said.

"There's not much food left, I'm afraid. There are a few chicken fingers, but we've not done the cake yet, so at least you can have some of that," Erica said.

An awkward silence fell between them, which Erica broke.

"Well, I guess we should do the cake now. I'll go and find a lighter to light the candles."

Once they were lit, she said, "C'mon, Benjamin! Come and sit up here at the table, so we can all sing 'Happy Birthday' to you. Then you can blow out the candles and make a wish."

Everyone was looking at her, but it was Carolina's eyes that pierced right through her as she said, "Thank you all for coming to help celebrate Benjamin's third birthday. Now if we could all sing 'Happy Birthday', that would be lovely."

This was ridiculous, Carolina's presence was making Erica feel uneasy, but she drove these thoughts away, feeling disgust with herself.

"Excuse me, sis, but I'd like to say a big thank you to you for making today so wonderful for Benjamin, and for making such an amazing cake.

"Let's raise a glass to Erica, before we do the cake," Frank said.

Afterwards, with the party being over, and the guests having scattered to their own homes, Erica felt content that the day's entertainment had gone well, but she wished that Carolina would hurry up and leave, so that she could relax with Frank and Laurence.

Erica studied her, listening to her carefully chosen words as she fingered the charm hanging from her necklace. Erica cringed. She really was a good-looking woman, but Laurence had been right about her; her beauty was only skin deep.

"You may not know this, Erica, but the impact Laurence has had on destroying my own and Benjamin's personal lives is beyond anything you can possibly imagine. I'm sure he rarely discusses how badly he treats us. I'm sure he's made himself out to be some type of saint and has painted me in a bad light. Well, that's not the truth."

"I'm sorry, but I don't want to hear this shit! Laurence is a very good friend of mine and has been for a very long time. How dare you say such words to me when my own husband was killed in an accident!"

"I'm impervious to your words, Carolina, and they are wholly inappropriate at our son's birthday party. I think you should leave now," Laurence said both gently and patiently.

Carolina's critical gaze swept over them all with a frown.

"C'mon, Benjamin. It's time we left. Mummy was never really welcome here anyway."

It was an ugly scene to watch, as Laurence scooped Benjamin up in his arms and kissed him goodbye.

"Don't forget! Daddy loves you."

Silently, Carolina seized Benjamin from Laurence's arms, took him by the hand and led him out of the front door.

"You did a superb job of not rising to her," Frank said as they heard the front door slam.

"Her mood swings are horrendous. She'll never change," Laurence replied.

Chapter 35

"Thank you so much for today, Erica. In return, I'd like to take you out tomorrow night for a meal."

"That would be lovely," she said, trying to lighten the mood.

"Thank goodness Benjamin didn't seem too concerned about the horrible end to his party. I think he had a fabulous day," Frank said.

"A lot has happened over the past few months. I think he's just used to the way his mother is," Laurence said as he rose from his seat.

"Good night, both. I'll collect you around seven tomorrow night, if that's okay with you, Erica?"

He touched her cheek gingerly as he left.

After Erica and Frank had cleared up and she'd made them supper, they were both so flummoxed by Laurence's situation with Carolina, and worried about Benjamin, that they just sat in silence with their own thoughts.

Retiring to her bedroom, she left her curtains open and lay on the bed staring at the full moon.

The following evening, sitting opposite Laurence in the restaurant, Erica couldn't help noticing how elegant he looked in his light grey suit, which accentuated his dark tan.

"It'd be nice to get away for a weekend, don't you think?" he asked.

She froze. Was he asking her to spend a weekend away with him?

"I'm sorry, Laurence, but for now at least, I think it'd be better if we didn't."

"Where's your logic in that? We could go as friends … separate bedrooms, and all that?"

"What if we took Benjamin with us? That would work for me," she said.

He laughed.

"Oh! So you think taking Benjamin with us would make me keep my distance from you?"

"No. I just think it would be nice for me to get to know him better, and we could do some fun family things."

"Actually, that would be lovely. I'll get it arranged. I guess my greatest fear is that he will grow up feeling disappointed in me."

Erica tucked in a stray lock of her hair and said graciously in a sweet but even-toned voice, "That won't happen. We'll make sure of that."

"I'm just so worried, with Carolina having primary custody of him, that at some point she may get difficult about my visitation rights."

"Surely, she realises that, at the end of the day, you'll always be his father. Just because your relationship has broken down, it doesn't mean she can ever take that position away from you."

Chapter 36

"This is wonderful," Erica said as Laurence drove, with Benjamin in his car seat in the rear.

"It's so nice to be getting away for the weekend with you both. I can't let you pay for everything, though. I intend to pay my way."

"I've never been to Norfolk before. It'll make a lovely change to go somewhere new," Laurence said.

"The forecast is for dry weather, so that's good news," she said.

Arriving at the Airbnb he'd booked for them, Erica jumped out of the car. The place was a complete surprise to her; he'd not given her any clues as to where they would be staying. She took in the wide porch, which stretched across the full width of the building, above which were two balconies with black wrought iron banisters that curved out gracefully.

"Oh! It's beautiful! What a fantastic place to stay for two nights," she shouted. "I can't wait to see inside."

Laurence gently removed Benjamin, who was fast asleep, from his car seat.

Erica's large eyes were clear and calm, the curves of her slender frame complemented by the cut of the new summer dress she was wearing.

They entered through the front door, and Erica closed it behind them.

The inside of the house was majestic, full of light with a wonderful energy, and very romantic.

'Thank goodness we have Benjamin in tow,' she thought to herself.

"It's beautiful. Thank you so much for organising this," she said.

"There's a pub about a four mile walk from here. It looks lovely on the photos I've seen. I thought maybe we could hike there this afternoon, have a couple of drinks and something to eat, and then either get a taxi or walk back, depending on how tired we are," he said.

"Sounds wonderful. Have you brought a carrier for Benjamin?" she asked.

An hour later, they set out to walk along the riverbank of the quiet waters of the River Bure.

"Is Uncle Frank not coming?" Benjamin asked.

"No, just Erica and Daddy. You have us all to yourself for the whole weekend," Laurence replied.

Benjamin chuckled.

"I like being carried in here, Daddy."

Laurence clasped Erica's hand, and feeling its comfort, she didn't pull away.

They pushed forward on their journey, an appetite developing for the drinks and meal that lay ahead.

Erica caught Laurence's eye and then looked pointedly at Benjamin, who had a huge smile on his face.

It was a special moment between the three of them.

Chapter 37

Arriving at the pub they took a bench table in the gardens, and Benjamin went to play in the children's play area nearby. Laurence grinned at Erica, allowing free rein to the dimples in his cheeks.

The setting by the river was glorious, and Erica smiled as a lady rode past them on a black horse.

"How appropriate that the pub should be called *'The Black Horse'*, and in the first couple of minutes of our sitting here, a black horse has ridden past us.

Laurence suggested he should get them all some drinks and also bring back the food menu. Erica gladly welcomed the idea, her appetite having increased hugely during their walk.

Whilst Laurence was at the bar, Benjamin ran

over to her, and she was touched when he reached out and held her hand.

"Did you see me come down the big slide?" he asked excitedly.

She gave him a cuddle, taking in his sweet scent and his warmth.

"I did! You were amazing! Are you going to do it again?"

Coming back with the drinks and the food menus, Laurence placed them on the table.

"I thought tomorrow, we could take Benjamin swimming. There's a little beach area further along the river. You did pack a costume didn't you?"

Smiling and raising her eyebrows, she said, "I did. You mentioned that Benjamin might want to go swimming."

"I'm a wizard!" Benjamin shouted, as he came down the slide once more.

A couple of hours passed with them drinking wine, and eating the food, which when it arrived was hearty and good. Erica was relieved to sense that no awkwardness existed between them.

"I bet it's lovely here in the winter … in the snow," Erica said. "When we get back, I'm going to give my tenants notice on my apartment. I'm well enough now to live on my own, and it'll be nice to start getting my life back on track. I'm just hoping it won't be too difficult for me with all the memories of Bryan that are in the place."

"I'm sure you'll be fine. Some people's minds break in ways we don't understand, but I agree you definitely seem well again. It's so lovely to see you smiling and happy."

Benjamin rushed over to them and paused for a moment to catch his breath.

"Can we go now?" he asked, gulping the rest of his orange juice from his glass.

"Of course, we can. But I'm stunned that you don't want to play anymore. You *must* be tired."

Back at the house, Erica watched as Laurence carried Benjamin upstairs to settle him into bed. All she could feel was admiration for the man.

Afterwards he returned to her, Benjamin fast asleep in his bed. An odd energy flowed between them, and there was a silence for a long moment.

The ceiling fan above gave a light relief from the heat that she could feel rising within her body.

"I'll put some music on and open us a bottle

of wine," Laurence said, breaking the silence. Opening her mouth to respond, no words would surface.

"You can trust me, you know," Laurence said as he removed the cork from the bottle and poured them both a glass of red.

Her eyes widened, then ran over his body, appraising the situation.

Chapter 38

Before long, Erica found herself lying on the sofa, secure in Laurence's strong arms and wondering how she'd got there but knowing that a lot had happened in the last few moments.

He leant over and refilled her glass with wine.

Spending the rest of her lifetime on her own was not what she wanted, but was she ready to commit to him?

Part of her wished Benjamin would wake up, and the other part of her hoped he wouldn't.

"I love you," Laurence said with such sincerity in his voice that it brought tears to her eyes.

At that point, a curly blonde head with large blue eyes peeked around the door and said, "Daddy, I can't sleep. My bed feels strange. Can I sleep with you, please?"

Unravelling his arms from Erica, Laurence stood up and said, "C'mon. Let's get you some warm milk. And, yes. Of course, you can sleep with me."

He made a gesture with his hand to Erica, which she interpreted as 'sorry'.

The following morning, Erica grabbed a towel and turned on the shower in her en-suite.

Once downstairs, she found Laurence and Benjamin curled up together on the sofa, watching TV.

She smiled. Benjamin had offered her the perfect way out of a situation she still wasn't sure she was ready for.

What was Laurence to her? A friend, certainly. But their relationship was also romantic, so best friend didn't seem like a good description either.

"Morning! Would you both like a bacon sandwich for breakfast?" she asked.

"That would be lovely. Thank you," Laurence replied.

After spending a pleasant morning together, they headed out in Laurence's car to find the spot he had described the day before. As they took a sharp turn at the bottom of probably the only hill in The Broads, they came upon it.

A PARALLEL PERSONA

The mood between them all was playful as they splashed around together at the river edge. After drying off and changing back into their clothes, they drove until they found a perfect picnic spot, where they ate the fruit and pastries that Laurence had packed for them.

Afterwards, Erica lay back on a blanket, appreciating the sounds of the English countryside, whilst the boys played football.

An hour later, they packed everything away into the car, Erica's state of mind feeling comfortable as they drove back towards the house at Cripple Creek, with Benjamin chuckling in his car seat.

Chapter 39

Having crept downstairs after settling Benjamin into his own bed for the night, Laurence found Erica in the rear garden sipping a wine on the patio. He formed the OK sign with his fingers and winked.

"Do you need a top up? I'll just get myself a glass."

He lowered himself into the chair next to her.

"I feel truly blessed. This has been a fabulous weekend. Thank you for sharing it with Benjamin and me."

"I've enjoyed it. It's been lovely to have someone to talk to ... someone who understands. It's strange, you know, how I can't recall most of the time when I was ill. It's as though I've lost all of that time of my life."

"You still reminded me of the Erica we knew and loved, but we'd lost you to another world somehow."

"I'd lost my mind, I guess."

She gave him a slow smile.

"It was a frightening experience for us all," he said.

"Do you want to eat inside or outside? I'll lay the table. Dinner's almost ready," she said.

"Outside will be fine. I'll leave the back door open, just in case Benjamin finds his way downstairs again."

She laughed.

"Well, he did save the day, didn't he? Who knows what might have happened if he hadn't come down when he did last night?"

"I'll grab us a couple of blankets in case it goes chilly later. It's so lovely out here; we should make the most of it," he said.

Erica hurried inside to grab the stuff she needed for the table, her mind reeling and her body buzzing with the weird energy of the innuendo she had just thrown out at Laurence.

After dinner, they spent a quiet and relaxed evening together, sitting outside, blankets wrapped around their legs to keep out the chill, the conversation flowing easily between them.

A touch of humour lurked in Laurence's blue

eyes as he said, "Well, I don't know about you, but I'm shattered. Can I at least give you a goodnight kiss?"

Erica breathed in the clean air of the countryside and allowed him to kiss her briefly.

"Goodnight! And thank you for a lovely day," she said.

A few months later, it was time for Erica to leave Frank's home and move back into the sanctuary of her own apartment.

Donning a t-shirt and jeans, she crammed the last of her belongings into the oversized suitcase Frank had lent her.

She sat on the bed and looked around the bedroom, which had been her safety net for the last six months. The full impact of what she was about to do knocked her back slightly, so she took a minute to calm her nerves.

Both Frank and Laurence had offered to help her move in, and whilst she didn't have much to transport because the apartment had been let fully furnished, she was still grateful to them for their support.

Bryan's whisper reached out to her around the room.

"You can do this! C'mon! You'll be fine."

Closing her eyes, she tried to breathe him in. Mingled memories surfaced in her vision. She opened her eyes quickly; she wasn't going to allow her mind to travel into crisis again. It was time to let go.

"Now for the next chapter of my life," she said to herself.

Chapter 40

Erica entered the front door of her apartment, the very threshold Bryan had carried her over on their wedding night. Frank and Laurence followed her in.

Laurence headed straight to the fire in the lounge and lit it, to take off the chill of the wintry day.

Moving around from room to room, Erica wanted to take in every inch of this apartment that she so loved.

After inviting them both to stay for lunch, she stood in her own kitchen, and stirred the potato salad thoughtfully.

A few minutes later, Frank and Laurence came in and took their places at the kitchen table. They both took a keen interest in listening to Erica's plans about how she was going to move forward with the opening of her restaurant.

Cheered by the sight of such a lovely lunch, they dug in. For a moment, Erica studied Laurence's face, waiting for his response.

"I think you're onto a winner. I believed in you before, and I still feel you have a passion for this venture. I've every reason to think it will be a great success," he said.

"I'm happy to look over your finances and check that you have enough capital to go ahead," Frank said.

"Finding the right venue and energetic people to work for you is vital," Laurence added.

"I've been weighing up all of my options for a while now. I'm convinced I can make it work," she said.

The rest of their lunch break was spent brainstorming ideas.

Summing up, Erica said, "So the first thing I need to do is find a suitable venue and redesign it to what I have in mind. I'd best get my running shoes on and get cracking."

"It's lovely to see you setting your feet down and getting life back under your control," Frank said.

She answered him with a grin.

"It's going to be a beautiful restaurant, just you wait and see."

And so, the following day, Erica's patient, diligent, painstaking, but thorough, search for a venue started in earnest.

Once her self-will took command, everything became straightforward.

Chapter 41

Erica stood up and shook the landlord's hand.

"So, we have a deal. That's wonderful. It doesn't look very restaurant-like at the moment but wait until you see how I'm going to transform it."

She gazed around at the bare room. A blank canvas! She couldn't have asked for more.

It had been an interesting conversation, albeit in her favour. She allowed herself a smile, pleased with how the negotiation had gone. It was now her responsibility to make this work. The location was superb … in the local town, and only a few miles away from her apartment.

She woke the next morning in the cool light of dawn, thoughts and ideas rushing through her head, and by the end of the morning, she'd arranged a meeting with a reputable interior designer with plenty of experience.

Her confidence was growing by the minute as the woman said, "I can see you this afternoon. I've just had a cancellation."

A few hours later, Erica walked out of the offices of the interior design company feeling exhilarated and overjoyed that the meeting had gone so well. She was thrilled that her own ideas had been met so enthusiastically by the designer, down to the minutest of detail.

A couple of weeks later, the refurbishment started, and Erica began the interviewing process for her staff. Crucially, she knew that to get the perfect chef was paramount, whilst she herself would take on the front-of-house role, with an assistant to allow her to have time off occasionally.

The front of the restaurant had been barricaded off with bright yellow safety railings, so she arranged for the interviews to take place in a nearby coffee shop.

Three of the chefs she had shortlisted had come with superb letters of recommendation from former employers and clients.

The first one she interviewed was like Prince Charming himself, but he was a little too suave for her liking.

The second one, she asked, "So why should I employ you?"

He studied her face with amused eyes, and told her, "Because I'm the best."

He lost her at that point.

The third one, Archie, fitted the role just like a fairy tale fantasy. He was pure magic, representing everything she had dreamed of.

Understanding the success of the restaurant lay mainly in the quality of the food, so she asked Archie to come to her apartment the following evening to cook for Frank, Laurence and herself, with the prospect of being offered the job, should he satisfy her requirements.

Archie arrived right on time, wired with energy. She explained what she required from him for the three-course dinner for three.

He busied himself in the kitchen immediately, whilst she went to change into something more suitable for dinner, pleased with herself that she'd had the courage to speak to him in the manner she had, as his potential new boss.

The proof of whether she had chosen the right chef would now be in how good it tasted and how quickly they demolished the food he presented before them.

Chapter 42

Erica had chosen to go for a smart, but casual, look for dinner.

She wouldn't feel completely at peace until Archie had proved he could deliver the quality of food she expected. He had a high opinion of his standards, and she hoped he was able to live up to them.

Although she still had money put aside, Frank had explained, after looking at her finances, that she would need to break even fairly quickly if the restaurant was to be viable.

Despite having almost died of a broken heart, she was adamant that she was capable of doing this. She was going to take this responsibility, seriously.

She laid the dining room table and looked around her. She felt relieved that she'd decided to stay here, in this apartment, which she'd shared with Bryan. She'd proved to herself that she could now take care of herself; she'd be okay alone.

A dull ache had now replaced the sharp pain of missing Bryan. She ran her hand along the wood of the graceful dining table and was struck by the memory of choosing it with him. The wound was healing slowly; the harsh reality was now not quite so raw.

The winter wind whistled and rattled at the window, trying to seek a port of entry. She questioned in her mind if she should check on Archie in the kitchen but decided against it as he might see it as interfering. Instead, she settled down with a glass of wine. It was a nice feeling to have nothing to do but wait for her guests to arrive.

Frank arrived first, a beautiful bunch of lilies in hand, which he handed to her as he embraced her in a hug.

He took a seat and relaxed immediately as Erica poured him a glass of wine.

"So good to see you working so hard to reach your goals. Do you need to go and assist your chef, or will he be cooking alone?"

"I'm leaving him to it. I want to see what his presentation skills are like, as well as his cooking abilities."

The conversation continued to run freely between them until Laurence arrived.

Erica let Archie know that they were seated and ready for their first course.

The pumpkin soup lived up to the fantasy, and she was thrilled with both the taste and the presentation. The time passed pleasantly, and the conversation veered towards literature and history.

The second course proved that Archie was doing all he could to secure the job. The chat moved to Laurence discussing Benjamin and how he wished Carolina would be more amicable about the whole situation.

"Let's talk about something else," Erica suggested. "You're clearly getting upset about Benjamin."

"I just wish she didn't want to fight me over everything to do with him," Laurence said.

Archie entered with the desserts, which showed off his imagination and creativity.

After one spoonful, she knew she'd definitely found her chef.

Chapter 43

Over the course of the next few weeks, a lot of decisions had to be made about the opening and running of the restaurant.

It was now the day before the opening night and Erica had invited Frank and Laurence to the restaurant to show off everything that she had achieved. She laid down a tray full of warm scones and strawberry conserve on the table before them.

"So what do you both think?" she asked.

"I think you're a natural at this. It's incredible," Laurence replied.

"I always knew you were amazing, but I had no idea how well you'd be able to pull this off," Frank said.

Erica's eyes were smiling, and her face had taken on a childlike happiness.

"Even the rain drumming wildly on the roof

can't dampen my spirit. I'm just so excited for tomorrow evening."

Her eyes darted around the room, taking everything in, from the patches of pale blue sky on the ceiling visible through the artificial trees, to the pastel shades of the hanging flower clusters, and the flower garlands around the door frame and windows, with complementary real flowers adorning each of the tables.

"I already love my restaurant, and I'll fight as hard as I can to make it work," she said.

"I can't believe how good the trees look. You would think they were real," Laurence said.

"The old clocks and antique ornaments work well. You've done a fantastic job. I'm so proud of you," Frank said.

"I'm going to make tomorrow evening as much fun as I can. You're both still coming, aren't you?"

"Of course, we are. And we're both willing to help if need be," Laurence replied.

"My dream really is coming true, isn't it? I still can't quite believe it!" she said.

The following afternoon, Erica put on the sequined cocktail dress she'd bought especially for the occasion and headed over to her restaurant.

Archie opened the restaurant door, and she met his gaze with a smile.

"It's happening! It's really happening," she said.

Taking the fancy, cream-coloured, cotton tablecloths from the cupboard, she began to lay the tables. She placed a tall, perfectly designed, flower arrangement onto each one before laying out the cutlery. Adding a single, flickering cone of light was the final touch.

In spite of knowing it was too early for any patrons to arrive, she couldn't stop herself from glancing out of the window in the hope that Laurence or Frank might come sooner than expected, but the car park just contained her own and Archie's cars.

She turned away, not wanting to waste any more time.

The combination of excitement and adrenaline warmed her from the inside out.

Chapter 44

Archie joined her from the kitchen.

"It looks wonderful," he said.

"Indeed! I'm so happy, albeit a little nervous. Thank you so much for all your help. Do you feel confident that the kitchen will run smoothly?"

"It better had, or else I'll be bitterly disappointed with myself," he replied.

"Oh, the door! It's Laurence. I'll let you get back to the kitchen. Any problems call me."

Laurence's handsome face greeted her with a grin.

"Well, it's happening. Your opening night."

Erica felt warmth flood her face.

"I've seated you and Frank on the nearest table to the kitchen. I thought that, if Archie or I needed any help, then one of you could jump in … if that's okay?"

Laurence hesitated before taking the seat she'd offered him.

"Of course! Are you sure there's nothing I can do to help now? I have to say, the effect you have created here is unrivalled."

"It feels as though I've practically slept here for the past few weeks, but it's all been worth it."

"Well, it's amazing … as is your dress. You look fabulous," he said.

"Thank you. What would you like to drink? I'd love a glass of wine myself, but I daren't have one until the last customer leaves."

"I would love for you to choose for me," he replied.

A tenderness and love for him welled up inside her. He truly was a great friend.

She selected a bottle of red wine and poured him a glass.

"Not long now! I've just a few more details to check."

Frank arrived soon afterwards, and Erica showed him to the table he'd be sharing with Laurence.

Other patrons began to arrive, and Erica

greeted them all with her radiant smile, soaking up the compliments she received as they gasped in awe at the restaurant's beautiful interior decor.

The restaurant was soon in full swing. Erica rarely had time to think about how it was all going, as she rushed around making sure that all of her patrons were satisfied and happy.

It couldn't have gone better. The evening had been a total success, and after closing the door behind the last customer, Erica sat down with Laurence and Frank and poured them all a celebratory glass of champagne.

After a couple of minutes, Archie joined them. He'd proved himself to be an exceptional chef, albeit with a slightly fiery temper, as Erica had discovered when she'd witnessed a few expletives being thrown around the kitchen at times.

Laurence stood and raised his glass.

"Congratulations! What a fabulous opening night. Well done!"

Chapter 45

A month passed with the restaurant proving itself to be exceedingly popular. Every table was fully booked for just under five weeks in advance.

Laurence had asked Erica to take a rare night off for her birthday and she'd happily agreed. He collected her in his car, and they headed off out of town, down country lanes that took her back to childhood memories of barefoot strolls down dusty lanes with him.

"I love being in the countryside. It reminds me of when we were growing up together. They were such carefree days," she said, studying his face carefully as he drove.

"We did. Playing in the meadows, the haystacks and the river. Such happy memories."

He indicated left and drove into the small

gravel car park of a country pub. They entered and were ushered to a table next to a fire, which burned brightly in the fireplace, and once he returned from the bar with their drinks, they both ordered fish and chips. Music played quietly in the background.

"I value your friendship, Laurence. Thank you for bringing me out on my birthday. I've not had a night off in a whole month."

Leaning over the table, he touched her hand and that same-old, familiar warmth flashed through her.

The waiter interrupted their conversation as he placed the food they'd ordered on the table.

As he moved away, Laurence said, "I'll always be here to protect you, you know."

He handed her a gift box wrapped with ribbons.

"Happy birthday, Erica," he said with a smile.

She carefully unwrapped the ribbons.

"Thank you … but you didn't need to get me anything."

Inside was the most beautiful handmade necklace.

"Oh, Laurence! It's beautiful. I love it. What are the stones?"

"Malachite Topaz. I'm glad you like it."

"Thank you so much. Can you put it on for me, please?"

Erica lifted her hair from behind her neck and Laurence placed the necklace and fastened the clasp. As his fingers brushed against her skin, she felt the strength of his sturdy build.

Suddenly, it was as though she saw him through a different lens, her view on their relationship was shifting. She wanted him to kiss her, to make love to her, to commit to a future together.

He sat back down and watched her face.

"What is it? What do you want to say?"

His hand reached out for hers across the table.

Never in her wildest dreams could she just come out and say where her thoughts had led her. She removed her hand from his and continued to eat her meal.

Laurence's kind face held a hint of sympathy.

"Are you okay?"

"Erica?" he said in a tender voice and leant across the table and kissed the top of her head.

"I'm attracted to you, Laurence, but now I know it's more than that. I've fallen in love with you."

He reached across the table and took her hand once more.

"I've always wanted a lot more from you than just friendship. I'm madly in love with you. Will you spend the night at mine tonight?"

Her face lit up, full of relief that he felt the same way.

"I'd love to," she whispered.

About The Author

S.J.Gibbs is the co-author of *My Rachel* and *The Secrets To Healing With Clear Quartz Crystals.*

The Cutting Edge was her debut novel and *A Parallel Persona* is her second..

Her short story *Fighting A Battle With Himself* has been published.

She lives in a West Midlands village with her family and two dogs.

Printed in Great Britain
by Amazon

62802679R00192